How to leave the nest without alarming the Mama Bird:

Parental Perception: You're still their little girl, going off to face a big bad world—alone.

Reality: You're thirty-two, single and haven't sucked your thumb in years.

Tip: Make your parents proud. Take your ragged teddy bear with you.

Parental Perception: You'll starve to death before week's end.

Reality: You have enough chocolate to start your own candy shop.

Tip: Accept the groceries they pack for you. It's just better that way.

Parental Perception: You'll have no one to contact in case of emergency.

Reality: You haven't been to the doctor since your school shots.

Tip: Promise you'll wear a medical ID bracelet.

Parental Perception: You'll become a hermit. Thus, no grandchildren.

Reality: Guys aren't exactly knocking down your door.

Tip: Assure parents that at the first sign of Hunky Boy, you'll schedule the church.

Books by Diann Walker

Love Inspired

A Match Made in Bliss #341
Blissfully Yours #351

*Bliss Village

DIANN WALKER

and her husband, Jim, started on a three-mile trek through Amish country in 1997, and at that moment, she had no idea she was taking her first steps toward a new career. Inspired by their walk, she wrote an article, which was published a year later. Other articles soon followed. After studying fiction writing, she celebrated her first novella sale in 2001, with CBA bestselling novellas and novels, written as Diann Hunt, reaching the bookshelves soon afterward. Wanting to be used by God in the ministry of writing, Diann left her job as a court reporter in the fall of 2003 and now devotes her time to writing. Well, writing and spoiling her four granddaughters. She has been happily married forever and loves her family, chocolate, her friends, chocolate, her dog and, well, chocolate. Be sure to check out her Web site at www.diannhunt.com. Sign her guestbook and drop her an e-mail. And, hey, if you have any chocolate…

BLISSFULLY YOURS
DIANN WALKER

Steeple
Hill®

Published by Steeple Hill Books™

STEEPLE HILL BOOKS

Steeple
Hill®

ISBN 0-373-81265-5

BLISSFULLY YOURS

www.SteepleHill.com

Printed in U.S.A.

Delight yourself in the Lord, and He will give you the desires of your heart.
—*Psalms* 37:4

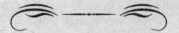

Special thanks to:

My fabulous editor, Krista Stroever, for the challenges and encouragement along the way. Your response time is amazing and your comments are always helpful. I am blessed to work with you.

My writing buddies, aka coffeehouse friends, Colleen Coble, Kristin Billerbeck and Denise Hunter. I value your advice, and above all, your friendship.

Jim, I am forever Blissfully Yours.

Chapter One

"Come on, Gwen, what better way to start off the New Year? This is a perfect job for you!" Candace Windsor says with more enthusiasm than I'm feeling. She tucks a strand of long blond hair behind her ear and smiles.

Lauren Cantrell sits beside Candace, nodding and stirring her coffee. "It would be so much fun to have you living in Bliss Village, Gwen. We could go shopping together, out for coffee—it would be great."

"And with me living in Nevada and both of you here, the three of us could get together more often than once a year," Candace adds.

Sitting near the fireplace, I feel warm and toasty, despite the fact I see snowflakes falling outside the window. Pine logs perfume the air, an aroma with which I've become familiar in my annual treks to California's Bliss Village. The three of us have been meeting in this town every year since college graduation. Now that Lauren and Garrett Cantrell are married, we meet here at their bed-and-breakfast. This year I took some extra time off before Christmas break so I could be with them and still make it home in time for Christmas Day.

The whole idea makes my dizzy. I mean, I'm all for adventure and fun, but leave Tumbleweed, Arizona? My home for almost thirty-two years?

"Besides, with your parents traveling six months out of the year, you'll be bored stiff if you stay at home by yourself," Candace continues.

I hadn't seen that one coming. She's got a point. My parents retired at the end of the last school year and purchased a motor home in the fall, but I never dreamed they would use it for anything other than occasional vacations. Since I've dated most of the eligible bachelors in Tumbleweed, my parents have given up hope of ever having grandkids to bounce on their knees. By the time I get married, my parents will have knee replacements.

How many times has **Mom** reminded me that my biological clock is ticking and time is running out? As much as that comment annoys me, the thought of not hearing it for the next six months makes me sad. Before my mood dives south, though, I look up to see my two best friends staring at me with hopeful eyes.

I can do this, can't I? I mean, so what if I have to leave my familiar surroundings; life is all about stretching and growing, right? The twinge of excitement sparks and soon the thrill of a new experience sends a rush of adrenaline through my veins. "I have to admit the idea appeals to me." I think for a moment. "But what about my teaching position in Tumbleweed?"

Candace waves her hand in the air. "Arizona's educational system can do without you for a semester. Take a sabbatical. Didn't you say you went into teaching to please your parents? It's time to find out what Gwen wants for her life."

I will miss my church friends, but most of them are married, so it's not as though they need me. And Candace has given me something to think about. I don't really know what I want to do with my life. This seems the perfect opportunity to find out. Okay, I'm getting excited here. "This is all so—so—"

"Perfect?" Candace grins again. "Gwen, you know you are a party waiting to happen."

I feel a smidgen of pride with her comment. I've always enjoyed it that people think that about me.

"You love adventure, challenges. What's that you always say—"

"You can do anything you set your mind to, if you want it badly enough," Lauren says.

"That's it," Candace shouts, with a snap of her fingers.

I reach a hand up to fidget with my hoop earring, causing my colored bracelets to clink against one another. "I imagine your brother will have something to say about this," I point out. "After all, this is his ski resort."

Candace waves her index finger in the air. "Ah, but I'm co-owner. Besides, I know he still needs a cook, and if you fill the job, that's one less thing he has to worry about. You'd be perfect. You already have experience from working at that restaurant in Tumbleweed during the weekends."

Lauren grabs my hand. "Did I tell you he'd be coming for dinner tonight?"

My heart blips. My gum grinds to a halt. Party animal that I am, I still get all twisted up inside when it comes to men. I'm racking my brain to remember what Candace's brother looked like. He was never around for our get-togethers. I have seen snapshots of him and Candace, but it's been so long. If only I could place him….

Lauren and Candace laugh together.

"Oh, come on. I know Mitch has a past, but he isn't that bad," Candace teases.

"A past?" I gulp here.

"Well, with women. He's been a little, let's just say, indecisive at times," Candace says.

"As in leaves a trail of broken hearts?" I ask.

"Yes—but that's in the past. Mitch has really changed."

Of course his sister would want to believe the best. Not that it matters to me if he's a player. After all, we're merely talking about me working for him.

The doorbell rings. "Oh, that must be him now," Candace says, already rising to answer it.

It could be me, but this seems to be happening too fast. These two already have me moved. Can I do this? My adventurous side says, "Yes, do it!" My cautious side says, "Hold on, don't move too fast. Think this through." Yes, I love adventure. Yes, I was complaining that I went into teaching because my parents made a living working in education. Yes, I want to try something new, but move to Bliss Village? Leave my safety bubble behind? I don't know. It's taking a huge risk, and, well, I haven't taken many risks lately.

Okay, try none.

Candace and a tall, broad-shouldered man with dark blond hair walk into the room and come toward me. He could be the star of any action movie on the screen today. I want to ask for his autograph.

"Gwen, this is my brother, Mitch."

All reason leaves my brain the moment we lock eyes. I'm thinking the adventurous side of me will win out.

"Mitch, Gwen Sandler."

His hazel eyes twinkle, and I realize I'm gaping. I snap my mouth shut and manage a smile. His strong hand dwarfs my own and sends sparks clear through me. *This* man needs a cook?

Just call me Betty Crocker.

My time with Candace and Lauren quickly drew to an end. Christmas is over, and I'm home packing to move to Bliss Village before the realization of what I'm doing can hit me.

"Gwen, are you sure you want to do this? I mean, if you're doing this because Dad and I are traveling…"

My top drawer gets stuck on something in the back. I yank out a stray yellow sock and shove the drawer closed. The cinnamon candle on the dresser flickers and sputters a moment. Have I mentioned I'm totally into cinnamon? I love the smell and taste of this priceless spice. It conjures up warm fuzzies in me. I think it's because it reminds me of Christmas. And, of course, not only does Christmas have great spiritual significance, but it also translates into social gatherings, food and fun.

I take a whiff of my favorite scent and turn to my mom. "No, Mom. I'm glad for you and Dad. I really am. This is good for me. I needed a little push from the nest." I smile outwardly but grimace inwardly. How pathetic is it that I'm thirty-two years old and still living at home?

Mom bites her lower lip, a gesture she does when she's unsure about something. "Well, if you're certain this is what you want to do…"

I walk over to the opened box and stuff my remaining socks to the side. My heart squeezes at the sight of Mom sitting on the bright blue-and-yellow comforters on my bed surrounded by fluffy matching pillows and shams. I look around the room. I've always loved the cheery yellow walls. I'll miss her, and I'll miss my room. But I'm ready for this.

I think.

"Mom, it's not the end of the world. I'm moving to Bliss Village, California, not Alaska." I take the last two sweaters from my dresser, one cherry red, the other dazzling purple with sparkles all over it, and add them to the nearly full box.

With downcast eyes, Mom nods. We're both struggling here. "We'll keep in touch, and of course we'll be back in Tumbleweed during the winter months," she says.

I'm pretty sure I hear a sniffle, but Mom

hides it well. She thinks a moment, and panic sharpens her eyes. "Oh, no! I'll never see those grandchildren now."

Mom can be a bit, well, dramatic at times. "Mom, in case you haven't noticed, there are no grandchildren. I'm not married, remember?" I wiggle my diamond-free left hand in her direction.

She stiffens and hikes her nose in the air. "It's only a matter of time."

I stare at her. My mom sometimes lives in a dream world, populated by dozens of grandchildren. Since my brother Spencer and I are both still single, she has to stay in her dream world to enjoy the grandkids. "I'm afraid I've exhausted my resources in Tumbleweed, Mom."

She brightens. "Is that why you're leaving? Do you know something I don't?" That's where I get my positive nature. Mom never loses hope that my perfect soul mate lurks right around the next corner.

The vision of Mitch Windsor hits me then quickly fades. "Nope. No man on the horizon. I'm simply spreading my wings." I fling my arms open wide and twirl once, causing my hair to lift with the breeze and my dangly earrings to dance.

Mom chuckles in spite of herself, yet concern shadows her face. I sit on the bed beside her and grab her hand. "Look, Mom, I've enjoyed being a teacher up to now, but honestly, I went into teaching because you and Dad wanted me to. It's not really what I want to do."

She hikes her nose a bit. "Well, education has provided a good living for our family."

"Oh, I know," I jump in eagerly. "And I'm thankful for that. I really am." I try to ease into the next comment. "Only I'm not convinced it's what I'm supposed to do with my life."

"But a cook in a ski lodge, Gwen? I should think you got your fill of cooking for a crowd working down at the Oasis Restaurant. I never understood why you used up your weekends working there. No wonder you've never found Mr. Right. You haven't had the time. And what about your college training?"

I know Mom's emotions are bouncing around the same as mine. We don't know whether to be excited about the future or cry about the past.

"It's not wasted. Education is never wasted," I say, parroting her familiar words. I get up, close the bulging box and pull packing tape across the top, sealing it shut. "I'll be doing something I truly enjoy." I smile.

Mom quirks an eyebrow. "We should have sent you to a three-month cooking school. It would have saved us some money."

My bubble refuses to burst. "I promise I'll

make you proud, Mom." Maybe I shouldn't go that far, but, well, I'm beginning to feel good about this decision. It feels right. "Candace has gone out of her way to get me this job with her brother. He's trying something new. I'm trying something new. This is a good thing."

Mom keeps staring a hole through me with those dark eyes. "I think Herbert likes you, Gwen," Mom says, making a last-ditch effort to keep me here.

I cringe at her reference to the owner of Tumbleweed's only bookstore. Herbert Caudell is thirty-nine years old, wears polyester pants and lives with his mother. I hold my breath. Wait. I'm thirty-two, and I live with my mother. That thought rocks my world for a moment. But I don't do polyester. I release my breath.

My pet iguana leaves his habitat and saunters onto the bed. Mom shoots straight up to a standing position and turns to him with a frown. "Well, he's one thing I won't miss."

Guacamole and I ignore her comment. I scoop him into my arms and rub his belly. I admit maybe owning a pet iguana is a little eccentric. When my brother presented Guacamole as a birthday gift to me four years ago, I had no idea what I would do with him. As we all know, an iguana is hardly the party animal. A white toy poodle dressed in pink bows and coats? Party animal. An iguana? No.

Still, I decided to make the most of it. He was a gift, after all. And green is one of my favorite colors. Besides, Guacamole's color reminds me of a dip, and, of course, where does one find dips? At parties. Once that realization hit me, Guacamole and I became fast friends.

Mom purses her lips together and heads for my bedroom door. "I've made you a lunch for your trip. Now you be sure and call us along the way so we know you're all right. I hate it that you're taking a loaded car by yourself. Everyone will know you're moving, and you're traveling alone."

"I'm taking clothes. We still have to see if this is going to work out before I move everything else."

My mom has always been a worrywart. That's another of our differences. I don't allow life's circumstances to get me all upset—well, most of the time I don't. I usually roll with the punches. Life is meant to be savored.

"I will call if I get into trouble, Mom. I promise."

"Well, before you go, your father and I have something to give you."

I look at Mom with surprise while she steps out of my room. I can't imagine what she's got up her sleeve. Probably a directory of eligible bachelors in Bliss Village.

Guacamole gets restless with my holding him, and he goes into his full-body alligator roll.

"If you don't want me to hold you, why don't you just say so?" I complain, watching Guacamole walk across the bed to a sunlit spot where he can do his usual basking. Oh, to have such a life.

I smooth the wrinkles on my bed where Mom had been sitting and wait on her return. She stumbles into my room, and I can't believe my eyes. There she stands with a broad smile on her face and a brand-new pair of top-of-the-line skis in one hand, a set of poles in the other.

"Just in case you decide to have some fun while you're there," Mom says. "I hear you can't go to Bliss Village without skis."

I take a hard look at the skis and wonder what I was thinking when I agreed to this.

Chapter Two

"Candace, I didn't know you would be here," I say as I stumble inside the Windsor Mountain B&B and Ski Resort with two suitcases.

"Here, let me help you." She holds the door, then once I'm inside, she lifts a suitcase from my grasp and puts it on the floor. "I had to finalize the joint venture paperwork with Mitch."

I drop my suitcase to the floor, brush the snow from my coat, then grab the slight bill on my black-and-red checkered hat and pull it off, along with my black gloves. "I can't believe I'm here," I say and turn to give her our customary hug. "Sorry, I'm all wet with snow." I brush the white flakes from my cap.

"After living here a while, you'll get used to it. Snow is a fact of life in Bliss Village," Candace says with a laugh.

Hearing that makes my stomach flip. "I have to admit I'm excited." I won't mention the part about not liking cold weather.

"You're going to love it here, Gwen. I have a feeling it will work out."

I have to wonder why she's so into this. Trying to help out a friend, I guess. That's the way things are between Candace, Lauren and me—we look out for each other.

"Hey, I like your hair cut that way, Gwen," she says.

I touch my brown hair, momentarily forgetting that I had it cut to shoulder length with some light layering. "Thanks."

I look around the room with pleasure and take a moment to catch my breath. I smell cinnamon from a nearby flickering candle. I'm thinking this could be a good sign.

"You like it?"

"It's incredible," I say, staring at the massive wooden beams, the stone fireplace, the rustic furnishings, spiral staircase, the wooden tables and chairs huddled on one side where, no doubt, breakfast is served. I think the room could use more color, mostly earth tones, but then that's just me.

Candace's gaze follows mine. "It is nice. Mitch has done a good job with it." She turns to me again. "You're excited—I can see it in your eyes."

Whether the excitement comes from the new adventure or the possibility of seeing Mitch again, I can't be sure. I have a suspicion, mind you, but time will tell.

"Come on, I'll show you to your room."

I pick up my luggage and follow Candace up the stairway to our left.

"Mitch isn't here. He had to run some errands," she says over her shoulder, reading my mind. "Your room is right near the stairway."

We get to the top of the stairs and walk three steps to our left. Candace places my luggage on the floor and opens the door with a key. She shoves the door open, steps back and lets me go in first.

Inside the room is a spacious bathroom, complete with shower, bath and ceramic tile flooring. A cathedral ceiling gives the bedroom a spacious feel. However, even though the room is very nice and simple, it's, well—beige has exploded all over the place. A king-size bed with a beige quilt hugs one beige wall, with two small stands on either side. An animal skin of some type hangs above it. Double doors from the opposite wall lead to a balcony patio. A small stone fireplace flanks the right wall. A small chair and stand with the telephone sit near the fireplace.

"Very pretty," I say, trying to hide my disappointment with the beige attack. My world is not the same without bright reds, yellows, greens and blues.

Candace shrugs. "It's nothing elaborate, but it is kind of cozy."

Maybe not elaborate color-wise, but everything looks comfortable. Candace's idea of elaborate and mine are two different things. We come from different worlds.

"Oh, dear, I almost forgot Guacamole. I have to get him from the car."

Candace smiles and bites her lip. "You know, I forgot to tell Mitch about Guacamole."

I stop. "Is that a problem?"

She shrugs. "Too late now."

She doesn't seem worried about it, so I figure it must be all right. I run down the stairs and out the door. Opening my car, I grab the handle of Guacamole's travel cage and decide to come back later for my packed boxes. I'm thankful I've wrapped a blanket around the bottom, or he'd be mad at me. Same as me, he hates the cold. I take him inside and up the stairs, where Candace is still waiting in my room.

Her eyebrows lift. "So this is Guacamole in the flesh."

"Yep," I say like the proud mama I am. "Haven't you seen him before?"

"Just pictures." I notice her face doesn't look

all that pleasant as she watches Guacamole shuffle around in his cage. The good news is his green body stands out in the room, and suddenly I'm thankful he's not a white poodle.

"I think you've found the perfect name." She laughs. "How long have you had him?"

"Guacamole is two years old. Iguanas can live as long as twenty years."

"Amazing. That takes true commitment."

I nod. "If I ever get married, the man will have to love Guacamole, too." I stick my fingers in Guacamole's cage and rub his tail. "I have a wooden habitat for him—looks similar to open bookshelves, complete with warming lights. But it's open in the front so he's free to roam. I hope that's all right."

Candace's eyebrows lift.

I can't help but laugh at her expression. "Guacamole is litter-trained, so you don't need to worry about, um, surprises."

She relaxes. "What does he eat?" she asks, still looking a little worried.

"Bedposts, wooden chairs. Now, he's not into pine wood. Mainly walnut, cherry, that kind of thing."

Candace's eyes grow large as snowballs.

"I'm kidding." I laugh. Candace's shoulders relax. "He eats healthier than I do. Staple veggies such as okra, green beans, butternut squash, acorn squash, mustard greens, some fruit occasionally—bananas, berries, peaches, pears, that kind of thing. Pretty much anything in the produce section," I say with a laugh. "You're sure your brother won't mind, right?"

"Oh, yeah, don't worry about it," Candace says with a lighthearted tone of voice.

We hear the front door open downstairs.

"I think that's Mitch."

My heart blips again. I put Guacamole's cage near the bed and follow Candace down the stairs. I glance at the banister and wonder for a fleeting second what it would be like to slide down it.

At the sight of Mitch, I struggle to breathe. My teeth stick together as though I've got a wad of saltwater taffy in my mouth. His thick, wavy hair is pushed away from his forehead with a bit of gel, and stylish sideburns end where his chiseled jawline begins. There's not an ounce of fat on his body. The word buff comes to mind. I'm sure he must have been a football star at one time.

He extends his hand. "Hey, Gwen, good to see you again," he says, flashing a grin.

My teeth are still stuck together, so I merely smile and shake his hand. He looks at me kind of funny, and I realize I'm still grasping his hand. I reluctantly give it back to him. *Killjoy*.

We step away from the door so he can get through, though I'm very tempted to stay put so he has to move me himself. My teeth start to hurt, and I pry them apart.

Mitch steps into the great room, and we follow him.

"So you got everything taken care of at the bank?" Candace asks.

He nods. "I think we're almost ready for opening day." He casts a quick glance my way. "We do have one glitch, though."

I cast my prettiest smile and wonder what that could possibly have to do with me.

"Granny is coming tomorrow," he says to Candace.

Their eyes lock. "Granny Windsor?"

Judging by the look on Candace's face, I'm thinking this can't be good. Yoo-hoo, anyone want to fill me in here?

"Did she say how long she would be staying?"

"Well, you see, that's the thing," Mitch says. "She wanted to come and check out my new place. I told her it would be great to have her here. Then the next thing I knew she decided to be the cook for the B and B. I don't really know how that happened."

"That's Granny for you," Candace says, shaking her head.

Well, this is embarrassing. I've barely moved in, and I'm already laid off—before I cook my first meal. Can't somebody tell Granny I was here first?

"Mitch, you should have told her you had a cook already."

Hear, hear, Hunky Boy's sister wins the prize!

"I know," he says, running his fingers through his hair. I wish I could do that. "But with Grandpa's death and all, I think she needs to keep busy."

"Look, Mitch, your compassionate side sometimes goes against your better judgment. We all have struggles we need to work through. Granny will be all right."

I suddenly realize I'm eavesdropping on a family matter.

Candace turns to me. "Grandpa died about four months ago, and we're trying to help Granny through it. But don't let her fool you, she's a strong one. We have to watch her. She's usually up to something."

"She is ornery, but still I want to do what I can to help her." Mitch looks at me. "That is, I want to help Granny, but I don't mean to put you out, either. I was thinking you could run Cool Beanz, the coffeehouse, for us. Provide specialty coffees, Danish rolls, sandwiches and soft drinks, that kind of thing. We won't be serving real meals, other than breakfast, until the business grows and I can add a restaurant."

I'm feeling better. At least I still have a job. "Sure, I'd be glad to do that." I'm hoping this doesn't mean a decrease in pay. I'm already way under my teaching wage. And this is starting to feel like a game of limbo.

"I'll still pay you the same. You'll keep plenty busy. I have someone else lined up to help you, too." He gives me a reassuring smile, and I notice how even and white his teeth are. His lips are perfect, too. Not collagen-large or paper-thin. I've never liked men with thin lips. Just freaks me out to think about it.

"Where is Cool Beanz located?" I ask. I don't remember seeing a building like that before I came into the B and B.

Mitch plops down on the sofa. "Oh, it's at the top of the slope."

His words slash through my happy moment. I fall onto the sofa across from him. Great. The top of the mountain is encircled in a cloud. The thought of being up that high makes me gasp for breath.

"You all right?"

A Darth Vader sound has entered the room, and I suddenly realize it's coming from me. I attempt to swallow my fears and simply nod.

He studies me a minute. The look on his face makes my heart skip. "I saw your skis in the car. I figure with a nice set like that, you'll enjoy the trip down that slope." He gives me a sort of studly look as though he had something to do with the mountain being so high.

Mountain. I'll be working on top of a mountain. I'm trying to swallow here but I can't. Just won't happen. I'm wondering if this might be a good time to mention that whole vertigo thing. Or maybe my fear of heights. Better still, perhaps he would like to know that I don't ski. Actually, "never skied" would be the more appropriate response here.

He stretches his arm across the back of the sofa and smiles as though life couldn't get any better. "Candace, aside from the deal with Granny, things are perfect. I've never been so excited about anything in my life."

Maybe now is not the best time to tell him.

I look at his strong arm stretched across the sofa and imagine for only a moment what it would be like to snuggle in beside him.

"Hey, nice sweater," he says, pointing to my multicolored sweater of reds, yellows and blues.

"Thanks." The man appreciates color.

"Want some coffee?" Candace asks us both, already making her way toward the kitchen.

"Sounds great," Mitch says.

"Sure. You need some help?" I ask.

Candace waves me away. "You two get to know each other some more. I'll take care of the coffee."

I hear myself gulp, then I turn to Mitch and lift a weak smile.

Despite the snow outside, his hazel eyes warm me clear through. Maybe it's the fireplace that does it, but maybe not.

"We didn't get to talk all that much at Lauren and Garrett's the night we met."

Oh, I like the way he says, "The night we met."

"So, tell me more about yourself," he says with a grin that curls my toes.

Well, let's see, I'm thirty-two, single, and setting my sights on you, Big Guy. "I've been teaching fifth grade since I graduated from college. And as you know, I've worked part-time as a cook at the Oasis Restaurant back home."

"Candace tells me you're taking a sabbatical to try something new."

I nod.

"Well, I'm glad you're here," he says, eyes sparkling. My heart zips to my throat. "I hope this whole thing works out and you decide to stay on with me." His gaze shoots straight to my heart.

Did he say "Stay on with me"? Forget that whole "I hope this works out" thing. You name the date, babe, and I'm at the church. I put my left hand in full view in case he wants to check out my ring finger. Mom would be so proud.

Candace steps back into the room. "The coffee is brewing." She sits on the sofa beside me. "Gwen believes you can do anything you set your mind to, if you want it badly enough."

Mitch rubs his jaw. "Oh, really?"

I'm feeling a tad less confident than usual because of that whole coffeehouse on the mountain thing, but my bubbly side kicks in. "That's right. But of course, the key is in wanting it enough."

He smiles and scoots to the edge of his seat. With elbows on his knees, fingers clasped in front of him, he says, "That's so true, Gwen."

"Didn't I tell you that you would get along, Mitch?" Candace says with a wink.

"That you did," he says, his gaze never leaving my face. "Then you won't mind managing Cool Beanz for me?"

Is he kidding? I would climb Mount Everest for him. His smile mesmerizes me, and I almost swallow my tongue. "Oh, uh, no, that will be fine," I hear myself say. I'll get some DVDs, search the Internet for diagrams, do whatever it takes to get up and down that mountain, maybe even with skis. How hard can that be?

"Great!" He rubs his hands together eagerly.

"Be right back with the coffee," Candace says, heading once again to the kitchen.

I really want to tell them both that I don't ski. I mean, they haven't even asked me if I ski. I suppose they think everyone skis because they're from Bliss Village. People here probably give skis at baby showers.

Mitch's brows furrow. "I hope we continue to get snow late into the season."

"Doesn't it last a while in the mountains?" I'm wondering why he's worrying. It's not exactly Tumbleweed, Arizona, here.

He brightens. "Yeah, you're right." Smile back in place. My toes curl again. I'm beginning to feel like an elf.

Candace brings in the coffee and serves us. We settle in for a nice chat. "Don't forget about the New Year's party at Lauren and Garrett's tonight," she says.

My eyes lock with Mitch for an instant. I wonder if he's bringing a date.

"I'll be there," Mitch says happily.

"Me, too." I perk up.

"If I know Lauren, it should be fun," Candace says before sipping from her cup. "Say, Mitch, since you're not opening for a few days, are you going to give Gwen time to get to know the area?"

Mitch winks at Candace. "I think we can manage that," he says.

I'm thinking it would be nice if he took me around town.

"Well, with tomorrow being the start of a new year, everything will be closed. But you could check things out the following day. After that, you can look over our place, get acquainted with the area and Cool Beanz. Anything in particular you want to check out?" he asks.

Another swoosh of adrenaline. Maybe this is an offer. "Oh, I don't know yet," I say with a sheepish grin.

"Wish I could take you around, but time won't allow me. Last-minute details, you know."

"Sure," I say, though my heart plunges to my knees. Oh, well, the library might be a good place to start. Surely they have instructional DVDs on how to ski.

"You might want to saunter over to Dream Slopes and check out the competition," Candace says in her business voice. "Get acclimated with how things are done at a resort when it's open."

Mitch sits up again. "Say, that's a great idea, Candace." He looks back to me. "Dream Slopes is our closest competition. A ski resort about twenty miles down the road. Bigger than ours, but I'm hoping this place, being a bed-and-breakfast and all, will add a little more charm than the bigger resorts. We'll try to offer that neighborly touch as opposed to the big hotel chain feel."

"Great. I'll check it out," I say. And maybe I'll take a skiing lesson while I'm there....

Chapter Three

The bright morning light floods into my room, causing my eyelids to crack open. It takes me a full minute to get used to the idea that a new day has dawned. Still, with the holiday over, I'm looking forward to a brand-new day.

I spent all of yesterday unpacking and getting settled into my room. I also browsed through some ski books I found on a bookshelf downstairs. It had been a restful day, but I'm ready to check out the area now that it's back to business as usual.

Not wanting to get up yet, I stare at the ceiling. Thoughts of Lauren and Garrett's party make me smile, even though Mitch had not been able to stay long. Some last-minute detail for the business had cropped up, and he had to take care of it.

My fingertips explore the tangle of hair on my

head, and I groan. How can I work up such a snarl in one night?

Guacamole scoots around on the bathroom tile and pulls my attention to him. "Good morning, Guacamole," I call from my bed. He ignores me completely.

Reptiles can be so cold.

"Well, it's time to wake up and smell the coffee," I say, yanking off the down-filled comforters. I happily step into my red slippers and red polka-dotted robe, and walk over to the window. The view makes my breath stick in my throat. I think I'm on top of the world. Then I remember. Um, no, that would be where I'm going to work at the coffeehouse.

A blanket of white covers the mountain and distant slopes. Coming from the deserts of Arizona, I can hardly believe I'm here. Not to mention the mere thought of Mitch makes me drool. That usually only happens when I think of cashews. Yeah, I know. Most women crave chocolate and shopping. Now don't get me wrong. I love chocolate, too—would never turn it down, as a matter of fact. Still, if I had to choose between chocolate and cashews, well, chocolate would just lose, that's all. I'm thinking I have definite issues.

Allowing my mind to wander, I stare outside

when I suddenly realize someone is waving at me. To my horror, it's Mitch. He's dressed in a thick black coat and ski cap and doing that jock kind of quick hand wave. It makes my heart act as though I've skied down a two-mile run. All right, so I don't know anything about that, but I do know about the heart-racing thing. I jerk away from the window. Not only do I not want Mitch to see me, but I'm afraid a giant bald eagle will swoop down, crash through the window and take residence upon my head.

I walk into the bathroom, step around Guacamole, look into the mirror and try not to scream. The man who marries me will either need strong drugs in the morning—espresso straight up, venti size—or have a vision problem, as in, blind. I'm sure it's the only way we could cohabitate.

Unfortunately, I don't see Mitch Windsor qualifying for the position. "What's the matter with me? I mean, it's not as though I have a chance with this guy anyway," I say to Guacamole, who is checking out the shower stall. I look back at the mirror. "Besides, he will hate me once he discovers I'm a fair-weather, feet-on-the-ground kind of gal." I'm talking to myself in a mirror, and I have a bird's nest on my head. How good can this be? I sigh and seriously consider going back to bed.

I'm not officially reporting for duty today. Still, I can't be a slug. It's not in my nature.

I haven't really had a chance to visit Martha Windsor, Candace's granny, aka the new cook. She arrived last night, and I stayed in my room to give them some family time together. So I figure now might be a good time to get to know her. Once word gets out on the B and B, I suspect we'll be pretty busy.

After directing Guacamole back to his habitat—not that he'll stay there—I grab a bright green sweater and khaki pants, and head for the shower.

The scent of strong coffee and spicy sausage greets me as I descend the stairs. The polished wooden banister still calls out to me, but I ignore it. I am, after all, a grown woman.

Martha brings a tray of breakfast dishes to one of the tables in the great room, as Mitch walks through the front door. He walks into the dining area—his face red, and his eyes vibrant. "Good morning, sleepyhead," he teases me when he steps inside. I like that he teases me. At least, I think I do. I hope he doesn't think of me as a kid sister.

"Hi," I say with a smile.

Mitch pulls off his black gloves and rubs his hands together. "Granny, that looks great." He gives her a peck on the cheek.

Oh, I'll take one of those, I want to say, but of course, I keep silent.

"Mitch, you're cold," Granny says with a mock frown. "Get your coat off and come join us." She turns and stares at me, and to be honest, she doesn't look all that friendly.

"Hi, I'm Gwen Sandler," I say, extending my hand.

She shakes her head. "I've got to keep my hands clean while I'm handling the food. I hope you like sausage, biscuits and gravy, because that's all I'm fixing."

I look over at Mitch, who shrugs and offers an apologetic smile.

"I love it." Feeling a little nervous, I scoot into my chair. I watch as Martha lifts the dishes from the tray and arranges them on the table. I would help her, but I figure she'd go into this speech about the germs on my hands. I fold my hands and hide them on my lap. My fingers turn the colored bracelets on my right wrist, a habit I acquired shortly after my thumb-sucking days ended.

Soon the table is spread with a feast fit for a king.

"This looks fantastic, Granny," Mitch says.

She snaps her head forward. "Well, what did you expect? I've been cooking for fifty years." She throws me a look that says, "Try and top that one, sister."

I'm wondering if I've done something to offend her. I retrace my steps and can't imagine what. She hasn't known me long enough. She doesn't seem rude, really, just a granny with attitude. Sort of the Granny Clampett type. Come to think of it, she kind of resembles her, too. Hair pulled back in a tight bun, her body thin and wiry.

Out of the blue she says to me, "Don't call me Martha. Everybody calls me Granny." I almost see the hint of a smile here.

Mitch slips into his chair beside me. I shiver a moment for no reason at all. Well, except for the fact Mitch is so close I can smell his cologne. It reminds me of the great outdoors, fresh and energetic. Intoxicating. I want to lean into him and take a deep whiff, but then I remember my manners.

Without another word, Mitch and Granny join hands, then Mitch reaches for mine. They bow their heads, and he begins to pray for the meal. I try hard to concentrate on the prayer, I really do, but my palm is getting all sweaty, and I'm wondering if he'll notice. Plus I can feel the pulse in my fingers. And it's very fast. This is so embarrassing. He'll think I'm nervous, that I lack confidence. That I'm a wimp—or worse, that I have an artery problem.

I hear him say "amen," and I lift an apology heavenward for failing to participate in the prayer. I toss a quick smile to Mitch, hide my sweaty palm under the table and quickly wipe my hand on my khaki pants. Probably not the smartest thing I've ever done.

Granny picks up the plate of biscuits and passes them.

"So you're going to Dream Slopes this morning, you said?" Mitch asks as he takes a couple of biscuits and passes the plate to me.

"Thanks." My bracelets rattle as I take the plate. I remove one biscuit. I'd rather have three, but I want to appear the dainty female, even though I'm not. "Yeah. I wanted to check it out."

"Great," he says.

I feel proud that he's happy with my decision. Funny that it's important to me to please him. But after all, he is my boss.

He scoops some scrambled eggs onto his plate and smothers his biscuits with gravy. "They have a nice place, there's no denying that. But ours will be nicer." He looks at me and winks. "I'll take you to Cool Beanz when you get back."

I try to ignore the goose bumps crawling up my arm and take a tiny little bite from my naked biscuit. Did I mention I passed up the gravy? After the meal I think I'll sneak into the kitchen and lick the pan.

"Monica Howell does a fine job of running the place, but she doesn't always play by the rules," he says.

"Oh, don't tell me that girl is still up to her tricks." Granny spreads some jelly on her biscuit. "That one sure does need prayer," Granny says before taking a bite of her biscuit.

"I know," he says with a sigh. "Sometimes she gets me all stirred up, and prayer is the last thing I think about when it comes to Monica."

"From what your family has told me, she could try the patience of Job," Granny says.

They've piqued my interest in Monica. I'm wondering how old this woman is, what kind of personality she has, what she does that gets Mitch all stirred up.

He turns to me. "Monica is thirty-four, divorced and drop-dead gorgeous." Mitch must have read my mind.

Excuse me? Do I want to hear this? I'm thinking no.

"I went to school with her. But her charm is only on the outside, believe me."

Can anybody really be all that bad? I always believe the best in people. I can't help it. Innocent until proven guilty is my motto.

Granny and Mitch share a glance.

"See, in high school Monica and I dated. She never quite forgave me for losing interest and moving on. Still, we've maintained a civil relationship through the years. It doesn't help that I now have a business in direct competition with hers." He plops the last bite of biscuit in his mouth and shrugs. "That quote about a woman scorned sure is true."

"You got that right," Granny says with an ornery chuckle. "But in all fairness, from what I hear, she hasn't had it so easy."

"Yeah, must be tough growing up with all that wealth," he says with sarcasm.

Granny raises her eyebrows. "And you've lived in poverty?"

Mitch grins. "All right, so you've got me there."

I'm enjoying their conversation, even if I feel a little excluded at the moment.

"Enough about Monica." He wipes his mouth with a napkin. "Thanks for breakfast, Granny. It was delicious. I've got to get back out there and check the rope tow and ski lifts—make sure everything is running as smoothly as a beginner's slope." He scoots out his chair and puts his hand on my shoulder. "I'll see you in a little while." Putting on his coat, he grabs his hat and gloves and heads out the door.

My shoulder tingles where his fingers had been, and I linger there a moment.

"You want anything else?" Granny asks as she rises from her chair and starts to clear the table.

"No, thank you." I want to add that I'm stuffed

so she'll think I eat next to nothing, but that would be a flat-out lie. I'm not stuffed. I'm starving. I consider throwing myself on the biscuits and gravy, but decide against it. Instead, I lift some dishes to help clean off the table.

"Nope, this is my work," Granny says with a possessive edge to her voice.

My hands have been slapped so I will know my place around here. I'll have to work my way into her heart. In the meantime, I go to my room to get ready for my trip to Dream Slopes. Once inside, I see Guacamole nosing around the handbag that I had left on the floor. "Oh, no, you don't," I say, scooping it up. I have to keep everything out of his reach, or he'll hurt himself.

Which reminds me. I haven't told Mitch about Guacamole yet. Good grief. He doesn't know about my iguana. He probably won't mind, but an iguana is hardly a normal household pet. He also doesn't know I can't ski. The man will throw me out. I have to tell him. And soon.

The cold air stings my cheeks as I purchase my ski ticket at Dream Slopes and head for the entrance. My fingertips hide in my gloves and tingle from the chill.

Skiers and alpine trees dot the mountainside, giving the scene a winter wonderland feel to it.

The sky boasts a vibrant blue with only a smattering of shredded clouds drifting lazily along. God creates the most incredible color. I take a satisfying breath. Before leaving the B and B, I changed into my new purple ski suit, new gold-colored coat, gold-and-purple stretchy band around my head and matching ski gloves—complete with the leather strip for grabbing the rope tow. I feel quite the skier. My snow boots keep my feet warm as I trudge through the snow toward the rental building.

I could get into this. In fact, this is downright fun. The air invigorates my spirit, and I'm convinced I've done the right thing in taking this job. If I were back in Tumbleweed, I'd be in a stuffy old building, standing in front of a class of rowdy fifth graders, trying to make my voice be heard in hopes of teaching them a lesson or two.

I take a deep breath of the mountain air and feel thankful down to my toes. I think there's something to this whole mountaintop experience thing.

Once inside the rental building, I have to fill out some sort of card, giving my height, weight, experience as a skier, that type of thing. I'm not real excited about telling my weight to a total stranger. I mean, social security number is one thing, but weight? Anyway, the young woman looks nice enough, so I figure I can trust her not to spread the news.

She directs me to the next person, who looks over the card and looks at me as though I've lied about the weight thing. I didn't fudge, not even a little bit. I figure I'll never see these people again. Who cares if they know I'm not a size two? It's obvious anyway. With all these winter wraps on, almost everyone could be a candidate for plus-size clothes.

The woman directs me to the ski boots and then tells me how to proceed to get my skis. I admit it. I'm excited. This is totally out of character for me. Not the excited part, but the stepping out and doing something out of the ordinary. I mean, I enjoy a challenge, adventure, all that, but within the confines of my safety bubble. But away from home? Away from what I know and hold dear? That's a completely new adventure for me. A bit risky. Kind of scary and invigorating all at the same time.

I spot my ski boot size and pick up a pair that seem to match the weight of a cement truck. What do they put into these things? How can I possibly stand up in them? Deep breath, Gwen.

I find an empty spot on a nearby bench, sit down and pluck off my snow boots. Then I shrug on the ski boots. I strap them tightly around my ankles, and I wonder if my legs will turn purple.

I'll never know since I'm wearing purple pants. I look around to make sure no one is watching, and then I attempt to stand. Success. I don't even wobble—okay, maybe a little. Dragging my feet along, I slog over to the ski station with all the grace of Igor.

A middle-aged woman with rosy cheeks and large, brown-framed glasses greets me with a smile. I hand her my little paper with the pertinent information. She reads it, then walks over to a row of skis, and lifts a pair from the slats. I could have brought my own skis, but I want to see how they do things in the rental building and all, so I decide to play the tourist for now. She then goes over and retrieves a set of poles and brings everything to me. "Here you go," she says brightly.

"Thank you." I almost fall over with the awkwardness of the skis, the poles and the heavy boots. I smile my apology and trudge out of the way. I have to not only stay up in these boots, but I have to carry all this stuff?

I like challenges, I like challenges, I repeat over in my mind.

Finally, I make my way through the exit and step into the bright sunshine once again. My heart feels lighter, despite my concrete boots.

I see some workers standing nearby and

manage to approach them. "I'm interested in a private lesson. Who would I talk to about that?"

A dark-haired man in his thirties with chin stubble and a glint in his eye smiles brightly. "I can help you with that," he says. He takes my credit card to pay for the lesson and, before I can blink, we begin.

The good news is the bunny slope is small, so my vertigo and fear of heights should be at a minimum. However, five minutes into the lesson, it becomes apparent to me that I'm in over my head.

I'm at Bliss Village, on top of a mountain— well, a hill on the mountain, but I'm at a ski resort, mind you, attempting to ski. That's right. Me. Gwen Sandler, wearing a pair of skis and actually considering going downhill in them.

Would somebody please call 911? I think an alien life form has taken over my body.

Chapter Four

My first trip up the rope tow nearly scares the living daylights out of me. I had visions of a gentle ride up a nice little hill. Um, no. Picture me grabbing hold of a rough, thick rope, being jerked forward and hanging on for dear life. I am convinced my grasp on said rope is the only thing standing between me and the afterlife.

Still, about halfway up the slope, I have to admit a sense of accomplishment overtakes me. When the wind hits my face, I feel like a kid on a bike who raises her arms from the handlebars and says, "Hey, look at me!" I feel so alive.

But when I see the top of the hill coming toward me at breakneck speed, I realize that could all change in a heartbeat.

Before I can consider what to do, I reach the top and let go in a flash, causing my backside to crash down with a thud. My instructor, whose name is Greg, skis up behind me.

Despite the pain, I laugh for a moment, figuring this is all part of the learning process.

"That's all right, Gwen. You did a great job," he says with encouragement.

I scramble to get up. Greg stares at me. I struggle once again to rise, my arms growing weaker by the minute, and nothing happens. With my eyes, I plead to him for help, but he continues to stare back at me. I'm at a definite disadvantage here, but once I get all this stuff off, he'd better run.

"Keep your skis perpendicular to the slope, put your poles to the side and push yourself up," Greg says.

Easy for him to say. I strive to do that, but somehow in all the grunting and moving, my skis get turned. By the time I get myself up, I wobble a couple of times, glance at Greg, who is exchanging a smile with a pretty skier standing close by, and before I know it, my instability thrusts me forward. I go sailing down the slope, arms and poles waving wildly in the air, my legs splitting so far apart, I could win a national cheerleading competition. My scream punctuates the air and people scramble to get out of my way. It seems an eternity, but I zip to the end of the slope and plop hard upon the ground, my derriere growing intensely uncomfortable by now.

People around me stare, point and laugh. Two thoughts come to mind.

I hate skiing.

I might have to hurt somebody.

"Uh-oh, did somebody forget the perpendicular ski thing?" Greg says, flashing his handsome smile.

Just how much do you enjoy those pearly whites, buster? My thoughts are turning ugly, and I need to rein them in. I merely smile and this time, he helps me up.

"Now, Gwen, we're going to try this again. Try to push your shins into the tongue of your boots, keep your knees bent. You forgot the snowplow/wedge position. Any time you feel yourself sliding downward, snowplow your skis. Remember, front tips are almost touching, back of skies bowed outward." He demonstrates.

I don't want to try this again. Ever. I'm cold, hungry and my arms are shaking. Still, I've paid for this lesson, and I've got to follow through. Besides, if I don't learn to ski and the ski lift at Windsor Mountain malfunctions, I'll have to stay in Cool Beanz all night on top of the mountain where bears and moose might decide to drop in for a late-night snack. I have to learn to ski.

Greg takes me through several more runs down

the hill, teaches me a few more tricks of the trade—
or tries to, anyway—and then our hour is up.

"Listen, I know this is your first time, but you
did a good job, really."

"Thanks," I say, knowing he's getting paid to
say those things.

"I would suggest you try to go down the
beginner slopes and get a feel for real skiing." His
smile is back in place.

I nod, say my goodbye and turn to look for the
flattest ground to scoot across. Forget the practice business, I want some lunch, and I want it
now. A little hot chocolate or a mocha sounds
pretty good, too.

It takes me a good half hour to get myself out
of all the skiing paraphernalia, retrieve my
handbag from my locker and head to my car—
with my dignity barely intact. I could have
stopped at their restaurant, but I figure when I'm
getting paid room and board, why pay for food
somewhere else? Besides, I need a nap.

"So how did it go?" Mitch asks, as I climb out
of my car. Is this guy eager to hear about the competition? Nervous? Worried?

"Oh fine. I did a little skiing," I say, confident
that I have not told a lie. I *did* do a little skiing.
Very little.

He looks worried. "I know their slopes are

bigger, better and all that." He looks around. "I think we'll do fine, though, don't you?"

"Absolutely," I assure him, as though I know what I'm talking about—which I don't. "Ours will be a cozy establishment," I say, feeling embarrassed that I said ours instead of his. He looks at me and flashes a grin.

"Please don't take this as harassment of any kind, but I'm really glad you're here, Gwen." He walks with me up to the B and B.

If this is harassment, baby, bring it on.

"Thanks."

I slip on a slight incline in the snow, and Mitch reaches out and grabs my arm to steady me. "So do you think you can be happy here?"

I try to gather my wits about me, but I can't get past the touch of his hand. I know he has his gloves on, but I still feel the heat of his hand.

I take a deep breath, stare at the snow and mentally shake myself. I have to tell him about the whole ski problem. "Mitch, listen, I need to talk to you about something."

"Yeah?"

"Hey, you two," Granny calls out the back door. "You'd better get in here. Your food is getting cold."

"We're coming, Granny." Mitch's hold on my arm tightens as he helps me through the snow so we can get inside quicker.

My heart sinks. I have to let him know that I can't ski, and I have to tell him about Guacamole. I hate to spring it on him before opening day. One thing for sure. He'll be furious with me no matter when he finds out.

"We'll have to talk later. When Granny ain't happy, ain't nobody happy," he says with a laugh.

It's nothing compared to how you're going to feel when I tell you what I have to tell you, I think to myself. Suddenly, I'm not as hungry as I thought I was.

I'm fairly miserable through lunch, picking at my food, wondering how I've gotten myself into this mess.

"What's the matter, aren't you hungry?" Granny asks, pointing to my hamburger minus two bites, and the full stack of chips and apple slices still on my plate.

I look at Mitch and see concern in his eyes. Though I hardly know him, I know that I don't want to hurt him. He can hardly wait for opening day, and I don't want to ruin it for him.

"I'm fine. Just not very hungry."

Mitch relaxes. "I'm meeting with the workers in a few minutes. That should take about an hour. We'll be going over last-minute details and such. They'll check out their equipment. After that I'll show you around, and take you to

Cool Beanz. You need to meet Lisa Jamison, the woman who will be working with you. She'll only be here on an as-needed basis, though. That's the best she can do since she already has another part-time job, and attends community college." He shrugs. "I'll take what I can get."

Obviously. He's hired a woman with a fear of heights.

"If things get really busy, we'll hire more help later."

I nod.

"Lisa will be training you. She's taken care of a lot of the setup, but you need to get started before the crowds roll in." He grins.

I was hoping to stall the inevitable by working on menu plans, taking inventory, placing orders and such at the B and B, but I guess that's not going to happen. I can do this. I *can* do this.

We finish eating our meal, and I'm praying for ways to tell him my, um, less than strong points.

Mitch wipes his mouth with his napkin and scoots away from the table. "Great meal, Granny." He turns to me. "I'll be back and get you in an hour."

I nod then look to Granny to offer help with cleaning things up but one look at her tells me she might hurt me. She shakes her head before I can say anything and starts clearing the dishes.

"I'll go up to my room for a while," I say.

"Take your time. I'll be back and get you," Mitch says. His words are soothing.

"Thanks." I trudge my way up the stairs and think this might be a good time for a word with the Lord.

"Moms whose kids are in school fill the positions needed in the rental building." Mitch's words come out in frosty puffs as we make our way around the mountain. He introduces me to the new employees along the way, we put on snow boots and skis, and I'm thinking life as I have always known it—you know, where you breathe and eat, that sort of thing—is about to come to an end.

Dressed in all the ski stuff, we shuffle toward the lift. "I've invited some friends to ski this afternoon so we can kind of have a trial run with all the workers here. Tomorrow will be much the same. Candace and I will wander about, making sure everything is in place and running smoothly," Mitch says, pointing to the various work stations.

I glance at the employees as they mill around the area. The place looks alive with business, and I can't help feeling excited for Mitch. Must be wonderful to live out a dream. I don't even know what my dream is.

I watch a lift float heavenward, and I gulp out loud. Fortunately, there's enough distraction that Mitch doesn't seem to notice.

I want to go home. To my Tumbleweed, Arizona, home.

Now.

My heart quickens, and I'm sure I will have a coronary right this very minute. My knees wobble, and I have to give myself a pep talk.

"You doing all right?" he asks.

This is my way out, and I know it. But how can I let him down at a time like this? He needs me, right? I can do this. "I'm fine." So maybe I've had better days, but why worry him?

He smiles, and I schlep directly behind him toward the ski lift. The lift looms ominously before me. Marie Antoinette comes to mind.

There must be a trick to getting onto these ski lifts. I'm praying whatever it is, I can do it, and quickly. Have I mentioned I'm a klutz? Not horribly, but I do have my moments. Right now I'm praying this isn't one of them.

The wind is still, almost as though creation is holding its breath. Mitch and I step up to board the ski lift. My pulse beats against my temple. My hands feel clammy inside my gloves, and I'm tempted to take them off, but fear holds me perfectly still.

It would be a cinch to board without the skis, but when you have contraptions the size of California redwoods attached to your feet, well, it changes things, that's all.

I dare a glance at Mitch. He's smiling and waving at friends. His eyes dance; his face glows. This lifestyle agrees with him. Me, on the other hand? Let me serve hot coffee, throw around a few balloons and I'm in my element.

"Here it comes," he announces, causing my stomach to flip.

I've seen people do this on TV. They step in place and allow the lift to scoop them on board. I watch Mitch, and he takes the same stance. I follow suit. The lift takes me unaware, but I'm on and that's half the battle. I hear Mitch let out a contented sigh.

"Isn't this great, Gwen? I'm actually running a ski resort here." He scans the area in almost disbelief. For a moment, I forget my worries and concentrate on him. I want this to work. He's a nice guy. I mean it. Aside from the fact he's gorgeous, and my heart somersaults with the sight of him, he's truly a nice guy.

"You've got a great place here, Mitch," I say, keeping my eyes on him and thinking how great it feels to sit next to him this way. True, I'm holding the bar in a death grip, but at least I'm sitting here. Hopefully, I can let go when the time comes to get off.

I finally look around, not down, mind you, but around. "You know, something else that would be cool is sleigh rides. I think kids would like it, and couples would enjoy it in the evening."

He smiles. "That's a good idea. I'll have to check into that. Oh, speaking of kids, I wanted to talk to you about Friday. Someone told me we may have a high school class coming in. Knowing how kids gravitate toward coffee shops, I'm thinking you'll be plenty busy. Lisa will be here to help you, and Candace said she could help with the schoolkids if you need her. She's not going home until Saturday."

I nod. I see the top of the slope approaching, and as long as I keep my eyes lifted forward, I think I can do this.

"Hey, look, somebody wiped out," Mitch says, pointing almost directly below us.

Without thinking, I follow his gaze downward and see a dot on the slope. The lift rocks a little with Mitch's movement. As I bend slightly to see the skier, I notice my dangling feet, and the reality of where I am and what I'm doing hits me like an avalanche. My pulse bangs hard against the backs of my eyes. I break into a cold sweat. Vertigo takes over. My right hand grabs the side of the lift while everything around me starts to spin. My left hand clutches Mitch's arm in a death grip.

"Gwen, what is it?"

I can't talk. Everything around me is spinning. I can't tell if I'm up or down, and I know we're approaching the top of the hill. I think I'm going to die. I've not written out a will yet. Guacamole will become a ward of the state.

"Gwen? What is it?"

"I—I—I'm going to be sick," I manage through clenched teeth.

"Sick?" He says the word as if I've hit him in the face with a snowball.

By now I'm terrified. I'm all out of balance. What if I slip forward? I hold my breath for fear the slightest whisper can cause me to fall. I try to focus on Mitch's face, which looks the way mine feels, but I can't stay there long. His face keeps swirling around me. I try to close my eyes.

"Hold on to me, Gwen. Do you want to get off at the top, or do you want to risk riding this back to where we got on?"

I feel myself slipping. My arms tingle; my neck is wet beneath my hair. The thin air makes me gasp for every breath.

"Gwen, hang on! I've got you." Mitch grabs me hard against him.

I'm going to fall. I know I'm going to fall. I should have stayed in my classroom, on the ground, on precious soil. I slip another notch. *Oh God, please help me.*

"We're getting off here. I've got you, Gwen. Everything will be all right."

I hear him, but his words blur with the clouds around me. His fingers press through the layers of my clothes and pinch my ribs. I clutch his leg.

Mitch must have motioned to the lift operator, because I sense that the lift has stopped, but things around me continue to spin.

"Come on, Gwen, let's get off here," Mitch says, trying to pry me loose from the lift.

"Don't touch me." I hear the sharp growl of my voice and wonder how that could have come from me. My mother would be appalled.

"Gwen, you have to let loose. You'll be fine. Let me help you."

The only way he can pry my fingers loose from the bar is to chop off my hand.

Mitch has jumped off the lift, and I'm almost doubled over sideways. "I'm not getting off. I want to go down to the base," I say. I can't stay up this high. I'll never make it. I'll freeze to death or fall, or even worse, become bear bait.

"Hey, you guys all right?" the operator wants to know.

"She's sick but wants to stay on and go to the base."

"You want to ride back with her?" he asks.

"Absolutely. I can't leave her alone this way," Mitch says.

"I'll start it up again and radio down to the attendant at the base. He can watch for you and stop the lift so you can get her off."

"Thanks, man."

I hear what they say, but I can't steady myself. My stomach's churning. I feel as though I'm trapped inside a kaleidoscope. Colors swirling all around me. Swirling, swirling.

"Can you lift up a little, Gwen?" Mitch's voice sounds distant—as though he's in a faraway tunnel.

I raise my head slightly, and he slips in, scooting me up farther. He puts his arm around me and grips me tight against his shoulder. Under difference circumstances, I could get into this.

It seems to take forever but finally the nightmare comes to a halt. Mitch gathers me into his arms and lifts me out. I feel him carry me away.

"What's wrong?" I hear Candace's skis swoosh up beside us. Her voice is tight with worry.

"I don't know. She's sick. Something happened in the lift. Probably the flu or something."

"Oh, no. Gwen, are you all right?"

I want to answer her, but my stomach, the dizziness, the spinning.

When we reach the B and B, the episode subsides. My world sits upright once more, and the avalanche in my stomach begins to quiet. Granny opens the door, and Mitch takes me to the sofa.

"I'll get her a warm cloth," Granny says, already scurrying off toward the bathroom.

I take some deep, cleansing breaths while my equilibrium levels out. Once my world is back to normal, it's confession time. "I've made a mess of everything." I pull my hands to my face.

"Hey, it's all right. You can't help it," Mitch says, smoothing the hair from my forehead. "Don't worry about it."

Candace pats my arm. "Gwen, honey, it's all right."

"You don't understand," I mumble between my fingers. "I should have told you." Reluctantly, I pull my hands away.

I see them exchange a glance then look at me. "I'm so sorry," I say.

"It's all right, Gwen," Mitch says, the look on his face making me almost willing to go through the whole vertigo thing again to keep him happy.

Almost.

Granny returns and places the warm cloth across my forehead.

"Gwen, what is it?" Candace asks, reminding me of what I have to say.

"I wanted to tell you. I really did. I even tried to tell you." *If You want to open the earth and swallow me whole right about now, Lord, I'm okay with that.*

Mitch smiles and pats my hand. "Tell me what, Gwen?"

I don't hear the ground crack, not even the slightest rumble. I guess I'm on my own here. I take a deep breath and look up at Mitch.

"I'm afraid of heights, I have vertigo, and until this morning, I'd never skied a day in my life."

Chapter Five

The knot in my throat grows with Mitch's ever widening eyes. I wish he'd say something. Anything.

"Vertigo?" He stares at the pine stand and says the word as though he expects the furniture to answer. He lifts his gaze to me. "Why didn't you tell me?"

"I tried to. I really did." I'm sure he'll never believe me. I might as well pack up and go home now. "Candace, I should have told you long ago, but I was too ashamed."

"Oh, Gwen, this is all my fault. I shouldn't have talked you into this," Candace says.

"Talked her into this? I thought you said she wanted this job."

Granny clucks her tongue and heads for the stairway

I don't like the look on Mitch's face. I feel a sibling storm approaching. I'm thinking I want to go back on the ski lift. On second thought, maybe not. But why would Candace tell Mitch I actually wanted this job? She sought me out because he needed a cook—or so I thought. 'Course, the fact that Granny showed up makes me a bit suspicious now.

"Did you have anything to do with Granny coming?" Mitch puts as much punch in his voice as a whisper will allow.

"No, Mitch, I promise," Candace says, drawing an X across her heart with her finger and raising her hand in a solemn pledge.

Mitch seems to believe her. He blows out a sigh. I know he's wondering where to go from here.

"Don't worry, Mitch, I'll pack my things and head for home. This is my problem, not yours."

He looks at me with those warm hazel eyes, and my heart melts down to my toes. "No, I don't want you to leave, Gwen. We'll get through this."

I'm enjoying this a whole lot. He doesn't want me to leave. He's willing to work with me here. This has to mean something, right? The fact that he needs someone in the coffee shop nags at me a little, but I push it aside.

"I can ride the ski lift as long as I don't look down," I offer as some sort of truce.

He brightens a little, and I'm feeling a surge of hope.

"You really think so?"

I nod eagerly.

"I don't know, Gwen," Candace says, looking all motherly and concerned.

"I can do it, Candace," I say, my gaze cutting off further discussion. She looks from me to Mitch, back to me. Her right eyebrow rises, and I'm almost certain I see the hint of a smile playing at the corners of her mouth. Yeah, she gets it.

"Well, if you think so. I hope you know what you're doing," she says, and I have the feeling she's talking about more than the ski lift here.

My eyes hold hers. "I think I do." We both turn to Mitch who looks totally oblivious to the under-lying messages. He's such a guy. But that's a good thing. I'm glad that he's a guy. And I'm glad that he's oblivious. It's just better that way.

He looks into my face. "So will you stay?" His voice is husky here, and it causes my skin to tingle. I don't want to read more into things than are there, but my female radar tells me he might be interested in me, too.

Bring out a bowl of cashews. It's time to cele-brate.

I glance at Candace, and she's struggling to keep the smile from her face. That's a good sign. She must think he's interested, too.

Definitely a cashews moment.

"If you're sure you want someone like me around, vertigo, fear of heights, beginning skier, then I'll stay." Maybe I'm pushing things. Did I have to make a list?

He touches my arm. "We'll work it out." Then as if he remembers his sister being there, he turns to Candace. "Won't we, Candy?"

I'd forgotten he called her Candy. How cute is that? This guy is something else.

Candace's mouth splits into a full-grown grin and she nods.

Before we can talk on it further, Granny's scream slices through the air. We look toward the upper level where we hear her voice and see her inching her way backward, eyes open wide, staring at the carpet. I'm thinking the cashews will have to wait.

Mitch jumps up and races toward the stairs. My gaze locks with Candace. We both blurt "Guacamole!" and scramble up the stairs right on Mitch's heels. We reach the second floor, and my stomach lurches. I *so* want my safety bubble.

"What the… How in the world… Where the—" Mitch stammers, staring at the iguana, whose tail is whipping across the floor like a broom with attitude.

Guacamole's body is arched and his dewlap—that thing that hangs beneath his chin—is extended. He's definitely not in a happy mood.

"I can explain everything," Candace blabbers while keeping her gaze fixed on Guacamole. Our circle widens as though we're making room for John Travolta's dance scene in *Saturday Night Fever.*

"Come on, Guacamole, it's all right, boy." I bend so he can see me and edge him back toward my room.

"You know this…this…thing?" Mitch asks, his deep voice rising in pitch.

I nod without looking away from Guacamole. "Come on, baby, you can do it," I soothe, thinking I'll pluck out the little reptile's scales one by one if he doesn't get into my room this very minute. Maybe I don't mean that, but let me say if I had a dewlap, it would pretty much resemble a full-blown balloon right about now.

I get Guacamole in the room and close the door behind him. I turn to the others and lift a sheepish smile. "Sorry about that." They stare daggers through me, as though I've committed a heinous crime.

Granny's white as a ghost. Her mouth is hanging open.

Candace jumps in before anyone can say

anything. "I told Gwen she could bring her, um, pet."

"This is your *pet?*" I can tell Mitch is totally reevaluating his earlier opinion of me.

"Yes." I could throttle my brother. If he had given me a poodle for my birthday, I wouldn't be having this discussion right now.

"I need to get back outside and tend to my guests. We'll talk about your *pet* later."

I'm in trouble. I can feel it.

"Do you feel well enough to run the shop?" he asks.

"Yes." I'm thankful that's still an option.

Mitch looks at me a little longer than necessary. "We'll talk tonight." He turns and runs down the stairs before I can utter a word.

Granny gives a "harrumph," and descends the stairs grumbling something about reptiles belonging in the wild and anyone with any sense would know that.

I look at Candace. She makes a face. "That didn't go real well, did it?"

I shake my head.

Candace puts her arm around my shoulder as we head back to my room. "Don't worry about it. They were both a little shocked, is all. They'll warm to Guacamole."

Somehow the words *warm* and *Guacamole* don't belong in the same sentence.

"How do you suppose he got out?" Candace asks, plopping down on my bed.

I look around. "I have no idea. I'm almost sure I closed my door." It creeps me out a little to think of how it might have happened.

Candace nods. "Well, I'd better get back to work." She pulls herself from my bed. "The only thing you need to concentrate on is how to get up to Cool Beanz without getting sick."

"Know a good therapist?"

She laughs then looks at me. "Do you think something in your past has caused this?"

"I'm not all that deep, so I doubt it."

Candace doesn't crack a smile. "Take care of yourself, Gwen." There goes that motherly thing again.

"I will."

She leaves me to figure it all out on my own. I notice Guacamole scoots into the bathroom where I can't see him. Sometimes he's so smart it scares me.

"Don't think that because I can't see you you're not in trouble," I call out. I can almost imagine his scaly mouth forming a smug little smile.

I settle onto my bed. What a day. Well, at least everything is out in the open now. Mitch knows about the vertigo, my fear of heights, Guacamole, everything.

If he doesn't send me packing now, he never will. Oh, I like the sounds of that. I don't allow myself the pleasure of lingering in that thought. The day's not over yet.

I say a quick prayer for help, and decide to get back out on the ski lift. That thought alone could make me throw up, but I have to do this. I have to prove myself worthy of staying on—at the resort, not the ski lift—especially after Guacamole's dramatic entrance. If I go back to Tumbleweed, and if Mom has her way about it, I'll be destined to a life with Herbert Caudell. A world of beige and polyester.

Bring on Windsor Mountain.

I poke my head into the bathroom and see that Guacamole is lying on the floor, back to me, head sideways so that I can see one half of his face. His eye turns in my direction, but he stays perfectly still. He's trying to ignore me. The little lizard.

"Don't think you've heard the last from me, young man." He turns away as though he couldn't care less. "I don't know how you got out of the room, but it won't happen again." I step into the hallway and pull my bedroom door securely closed behind me.

Once downstairs, I put my gloves and hat back

on, determined to make it to the top of the mountain if it kills me.

And it just might.

The sun shines down from a perfect blue sky. Great skiing weather…I think. I don't know anything about skiing, but I can tell it's a nice day, after all.

I thought I could tackle the ski lift right away, but I was wrong. I wander around outside for a while, trying to work up the nerve to ride it. Merely looking up at the coffee shop makes my stomach rumble. The tune of "Climb Every Mountain" runs through my mind, and I want to bang my head against a wall.

I have to get up there. It's important to Mitch that I get started training with Lisa. Though I don't see why she can't come down to the B and B and teach me. I guess that's not practical since I can hardly serve the customers from the B and B. I guess I have to take the plunge sometime. Oh, bad choice of words.

"Mitch won't care if you want to wait a while, Gwen. You don't have to do this today."

I turn to see Candace. "No use putting it off. I can't expect Lisa to do all the work simply because I have a fear of heights. If I can't do this, I'll have to leave. It's not fair to Mitch, otherwise. Besides, I need to prove to myself that I can do this."

"You want me to go with you?"

We both stare at the moving cars on the lift.

"You don't have to. I can do this," I say in an effort to convince myself.

She hooks her arm through mine. "Sure, you can—with a little help from your friend." I don't miss the fact that she's nudging me toward the lift, one step at a time. Some friend.

I take a deep breath.

"It will be all right, Gwen. Don't look down. Keep your eyes focused straight ahead. I'll be right by your side. You won't fall. I promise."

We're going up for a fun ride, right? Maybe if I had a bag of cashews, it would help. At the very least, I should be chewing cinnamon gum. We step closer.

"You still okay?" Candace searches my face.

I nod and smile as best I can. I swallow hard as we step into place, awaiting our turn.

"Hold on to my arm if that helps," she says.

I nod, not really wanting to talk right now. My bed sounds pretty good. Throw in a can of cashews, a little chocolate, and I'm good to go. That thought alone makes me feel better.

The ski lift edges closer and scoots us onboard. My heart skips a beat, and I clench my teeth. Keep focused ahead. Don't look down.

"I know you've had a rotten day so far, but I

have to say I admire you for trying to do this again so soon, Gwen. You're something else."

I know Candace is trying to make me feel all brave, but I would really love to get my feet on solid ground again. Keep focused. Keep focused. Completely ignore the fact that my feet could touch treetops. Ignore it, I say.

"I can tell my brother really likes you," she says.

Excuse me, but could you save this conversation for the coffee shop? Somehow I think I would enjoy it more there. Keep focused.

Farther up we go. I could reach out and touch a cloud, which, of course, I won't do. It could possibly land me in Heaven. I want to go there someday, but I was rather hoping it wouldn't be today. Keep focused.

Emotions swirl and churn with my stomach as we inch our way up the mountain until the ski lift dumps us out at the top. My legs tremble beneath me.

Once we're standing upright on level ground, Candace turns to me and grabs my shoulders. "You did it, Gwen! You did it!"

I look at the retreating ski lift and then back to her. "I did do it, didn't I?" Just lump me in with the Joan of Arcs of the world. One more giant step for mankind and all that.

"I knew you could do it." She's bragging on me

so much, I can almost hear the brass band playing as we march toward the brown building that's labeled Cool Beanz.

We step inside and the rich smell of espresso greets us, along with the whir of the cappuccino machine.

"That's Lisa Jamison," Candace says, nodding toward the woman behind the counter.

She looks nice enough. Short red hair that flips behind her ears, brown eyes, a dusting of freckles sprinkled across her nose. She's dressed in a royal blue sweater and matching striped pants. Not a smidgen of beige anywhere. I like her already.

Walking over to the counter, we wait for the machine noise to stop and for Lisa to finish making the drink for the customer in front of us. I watch her technique as she stirs the hot brew, attaches a dome lid, inserts the nozzle of the whipped-cream can in the hole of the lid and fills the inside of the dome with a cloud of cream. Makes my mouth water merely looking at it.

She gives the man his drink and turns to us. "Candace, right?" she says with a smile.

"Good memory. So how's it going today?"

Lisa looks around the room. "Not bad, really. 'Course, opening day I'm sure we'll really be hoppin'." She looks at me.

"Lisa, I want you to meet the woman who will

be running the shop. This is Gwen Sandler. Gwen, Lisa Jamison."

"Hi," we both say at the same time.

"You ready to get started?"

"Sure."

"Great. I'll show you the equipment, how to prepare a few specialty drinks, then we'll go over inventory and stuff like that."

I look to Candace. "Guess I'll see you later." I want to plead with her not to leave me up here, but if I die now, I've lived a good life.

Candace smiles. "Great. I'll head outside and see what I can do to help out there. Good luck, Gwen. Good to see you, Lisa. Thanks again for helping us."

"Glad to do it." She opens the counter gate so I can step into the barista's world, and she quickly sets to showing me the ropes.

"So tell me about yourself, Gwen. I hear you're from Arizona?" She's cleaning the milk off the cappuccino machine with a towel.

"Yeah, Tumbleweed, Arizona. I'm a fifth-grade teacher, but I've taken a sabbatical to try something new."

"Good for you. I always say never close the door to new experiences. I want everything life has to offer, no matter what the cost."

I smile, assuming she's talking about taking

risks. Something I struggle with a little bit. Maybe this girl will be good for me.

"So will you be working based upon how busy we are, or how does that work?" I ask.

"Excuse me. I'd like a skinny mocha, please," a blond-haired woman with a red nose and cheeks says.

I watch as Lisa rings up the sale on the register and sets to work on the drink. She carefully measures a shot of espresso, warms the milk with the machine, pours in the coffee and chocolate. After a dollop of whipped cream, she hands the drink to the customer then turns to me. "You want to try the next one?"

"Sure."

She explains the differences between some of the drinks. "Americano consists of shots of espresso and water, hot or cold. Lattes, mochas, those kinds of drinks have milk." She pauses a moment. "Oh, by the way, I forgot to answer your question. I'll be helping out on an as-needed basis when I'm available in between my own part-time job and school. I don't work much at the other job. Usually just eight hours a week, if that. I'm only taking fifteen hours at school and they're fairly easy classes, so I should be able to help out quite a bit around here. Plus, the money will come in handy."

"Good, I'll look forward to working with you,"

I say, meaning it. I'm making a new friend here. I need that, especially since Candace will be leaving in a couple of days.

She stares at me a moment, which unnerves me a little. Then she smiles. "I'll look forward to it, too."

Right then a man's voice calls from the counter. "Hi, Lisa. I'd like an Americano, please."

I recognize Mitch's voice and step into view so he can see me.

"Gwen?" His expression is a cross between surprise and sheer pleasure. "Could I talk to you a minute?"

I exchange a glance with Lisa and step away from the counter. I follow Mitch over to a private table. He puts his hand on my arm. "You're all right?" He stares intently into my eyes, and I feel that blip in my chest again.

"I'm doing fine."

"How did you get up here?"

"I took the ski lift." I'm practically rocking on my heels. I am woman, hear me roar.

"You are amazing," he says for my ears only, his eyes locked with mine.

Somebody gulps. I think it was me, but I'm not sure. My throat's awful dry. Can a person gulp with a dry throat? I try to swallow, but I can't. That can only mean one thing. Mitch gulped. Whoo-hoo, I'm having a great time here.

"You know, the reason I came here was I wanted to give you a walkie-talkie. That way I can reach you if I need to talk to you and you can get me if you need me," Mitch says, handing me a walkie-talkie.

We both know he's making an effort to watch over me here. It's like he's handed me a hospital blanket in case I need help, but I'm okay with that.

"Thanks." Feeling a little embarrassed, I glance up in time to see Lisa staring at us. The look on her face says she's interested in what's going on between us. Why? Does she care about Mitch, too? I hope not. I like him, yet I was hoping I had found a new friend. I don't want to have to choose between the two of them.

Mitch would win hands down.

Chapter Six

Dressed in a thick black sweater and ski pants, Mitch is ready to go when we sit down to breakfast the next day. Candace and I are still looking at the world through slits. We have a full hour before we have to get to our posts. I did manage to put on a temporary outfit for breakfast, consisting of a sparkly gold knit top and black pants, and I ran a brush through my hair. Fine. So I applied a little makeup, too. Um, and glittery gold nail polish.

The fireplace is lit, making the room all warm and cozy. I love that on a frosty morning. And trust me here, this place wrote the book on frosty mornings.

"I declare, Mitch, you'd think you were a kid going to his first day of school," Granny says, scooping eggs and hash browns onto his plate.

His teeth sparkle a brilliant white. I want to tell

someone to dim the lights, but I realize it's a new day and I have to adjust.

Mitch says a quick prayer—and I do mean quick, here. He talks as though he's already downed a pot of espresso, and I know that's not possible. Granny and the cappuccino machine are not on speaking terms. Unless it says "mountain grown" on the can, she refuses to make it.

"How can you be that bright and cheery first thing in the morning?" Candace wants to know. She puts a spoonful of mixed fruit on her plate. How does she eat like that? I've never understood her health nuttery. Has this woman never heard of fat grams, carbohydrates, chocolate? She so needs a life.

He shrugs.

Granny fills her own plate. "You ready for opening day?

"I'm as ready as I'll ever be," Mitch says.

"Well, you'd better be if you're going to compete with Monica." Granny isn't one to mince words.

"I think I can handle Monica Howell all right," Mitch says with a slight bite to his voice.

Candace looks at both of them. "Granny, Mitch has done a fine job of researching this business and pulling together a great first day. I've no doubt the business will do well."

Granny raises a pale, gnarled finger. "Well, he'd

better keep an eye on the competition, that's the truth of it."

Mitch shoves the last bite of toast in his mouth, leaving most of the food on his plate, and scoots his chair from the table without saying a word. Candace and I exchange a glance and keep eating. Mitch takes determined steps across the floor. The front door closes behind him with a definite slam.

"Wonder what's got him in a snit," Granny comments as if she truly has no clue.

"I think he's nervous today," Candace says.

Mitch does seem a little touchy. Candace must be right. No doubt he's feeling opening day jitters.

At this point I can feel Granny's gaze boring into me, and I look up.

"You'd better keep that scaly reptile locked away, too. If he gets in my kitchen, I'll make him into a purse!"

"Granny, that's not very nice," Candace says, trying to smother a giggle behind her hand.

I don't know whether to laugh or call the animal abuse hotline. I'm thinking she and Guacamole deserve each other. I eat the last of my oatmeal— and what color is oatmeal?—and excuse myself from the table. Heading up the stairs, I stop to greet the housekeeper. Sculpted with gel, her short black hair with blond tips flips out. Dressed in jeans and an oversized sweatshirt, she looks all of nineteen.

"Kaci Butler, right?"

"Right."

"Since we only talked briefly the other night, I wanted to make sure again that you're all right with Guacamole being loose in my room."

She gives me a cocky grin. "Remember, I told you that I grew up with a python in the house. I'm not afraid of reptiles." She pops her gum with attitude and stares at me through thick dark lashes.

"So you know iguanas can get a little agitated when a stranger comes near?"

"Yeah, know all about it. Don't worry."

She makes me feel like an old woman fretting over nothing. Is thirty-two old? I guess to a nineteen-year-old the answer would be yes. I want to say, "I'm past the braces, so deal with it," but then that wouldn't be very Christian. Instead I say, "Well, all right, if you're sure."

"Yep."

"Thanks."

She heads on down the stairs, and I go up to my room, all the while praying Guacamole doesn't weird out when he sees the stranger in my room.

I somehow managed yet another trip up the ski lift—this time with Lisa—and walked over to the coffee shop. There has been a steady stream of customers, and I have to admit I've enjoyed myself today. I love the smell of coffee, the whir of the machine, the friendly attitude of everyone who enters. 'Course, I could do without the gust of cold air that swishes into the room when the door opens, but I guess you can't have everything.

I restock the Danish rolls and tidy the counter.

"Gwen, I'll need two frappés, please," Lisa calls over her shoulder. She's working the register while I prepare the drinks, then after lunch we'll switch.

It's hard not to lick the frappé or whipped cream from my fingers, but somehow I manage. I serve the current customers with a smile. Right behind them I see Mitch enter the shop with a beautiful woman. Hello? Do I want to see this?

I quickly hide behind my machine and peek around the side. Mitch's face is red and all aglow. I'm hoping it's because of the mountain air and not because of the woman beside him, whoever she is.

"What's the matter, Jake, haven't you ever seen a woman before?" Lisa's voice growls to the man in line. He's one of the ski lift operators.

"Yeah, but not one that looks like that," he says, turning to the woman beside Mitch and definitely enjoying the view.

"You can stop drooling, lover boy. I'll tell you right now you don't have enough money in your bank account to snag that one."

We both turn to Lisa, anxious to find out what she knows about this woman.

He leans his whiskered face over the counter. "And how do you know that, princess?" He winks.

I try not to cringe. He's not exactly a prize catch here, but then who am I to talk?

She leans toward him, her eyes cold and daring. "Don't call me princess," she says with a snarl. "I know because that woman is Monica Howell. Plenty of guys in this town have tried to catch her, but she only has eyes for Mitch Windsor. Everybody who's lived here any time at all knows that."

He frowns and turns back to the couple. "By the looks of things, he's not fighting her all that hard."

My gaze darts to Mitch, who is laughing beside her. These people are definitely robbing me of my joyful self.

"So what do you want to drink?" The impatience in Lisa's voice is obvious.

"I want a tall, hot Americano."

Lisa stares at him. "Don't we all."

He smiles at her, and she rings up the sale while I prepare his drink. I give it to him and he walks away, still managing to get another look at Monica.

"Jake the jerk," Lisa says.

"You know him?"

"I go to school with him. He drives me crazy."

After talking to another couple, Mitch and Monica walk my way. I suddenly realize their names even sound good together. Mitch and Monica. They could have their towels monogrammed M&M. What could be better than that? Chocolate and the man you love all having the same initials?

My mood plunges when I realize *my* name is Gwen. Do Mitch and Gwen go together? G&M? Not unless you're a car.

"Lisa, Gwen," Mitch says. "I want to introduce you to Monica Howell."

"Hello," we say in unison.

Monica lifts silky black hair behind her shoulders, causing light to glint from her golden hoop earrings. Her blue eyes sparkle, and she flashes a Catherine Zeta-Jones smile. I glance at Mitch, who's glowing so much I could use him in my room as a night light. Hmm, now *there's* an idea.

"Lisa is going to school, working part-time at the coffee shop downtown and helping us out. Other than that she's pretty much bored," Mitch says, laughing at his own clever comment.

Monica smiles and quickly turns her gaze toward me.

"This is, uh—"

My mouth goes dry. His eyes glaze. "Gwen Sandler," I say, extending my hand. Why don't you just shoot me now?

"I was going to get to that," he teases. "Seriously, Gwen's saved us."

My spirit perks a teensy bit here.

"She was going to cook for me, but as you know, Granny came along, so Gwen has saved the day by working at Cool Beanz."

Wait. How did Monica know Granny came along? I thought he didn't care for this woman, yet he acts as though they have daily conversations.

She nods then her eyes scrutinize me a little too closely. "You know, you look familiar."

She probably saw me at Dream Slopes, trying, but failing, to ski. I merely smile. No need to give her any more information than necessary.

"I doubt if you know her. She's only recently moved here from Arizona."

"Oh, a desert flower," she says with the hint of a smile on her lips that never reaches her eyes. Something about the way she says that makes me feel I should defend myself.

"She's a flower, all right," Mitch says, rushing to my rescue.

Monica turns to him with a pout. "Not the

cactus type, I hope, all prickly and everything."
She turns to me and forces a chuckle.

I totally don't feel a part of this conversation,
but I smile good-naturedly, trying not to allow my
first impression of this woman to sway me forever.
We all say and do things we don't mean from time
to time. Maybe she's a little nervous about Mitch's
opening day being a success since she's the competition. Yeah, I'm sure that's it.

They give Lisa their orders, and I watch
Monica. Every guy in the room is watching her,
too, and she's aware of their gazes. She glances
at them each time she tosses her hair behind her
shoulders. When she talks, her eyes flitter about
as though she's looking for the nearest mirror or
nearest admirer. She likes being the center of attention, and she plans to keep it that way.

Something about her bothers me, and I don't
think it's jealousy—well, maybe there's a tiny
hint of that going on in the deepest recesses of my
heart, but I think it's more than that. I can't quite
put my finger on it.

"Gwen, did you hear what I said?" Lisa, Mitch
and Monica are all staring at me.

"Oh, I'm sorry, Lisa. What?"

"I said two hot mochas, one skinny, both with
whipped cream."

"Two hot mochas, one skinny, both with whipped

cream," I repeat and set to work. Yep, that pretty much sums them up. Wait. I thought Mitch liked Americanos. Why is he changing his drink to match hers? He's trying to please her—why? All right, I admit it. That thought makes me a little green.

Just call me Guacamole.

Candace and I plop on the sofa after dinner, coffee in hand. I've made drinks all day and still managed not to consume any myself until now. I curl my feet up underneath me. I'm bone tired. Though I do a lot of standing in my classroom, I also do a lot of sitting at my desk while the students work on their lessons. Today was nothing but standing.

We ran through the inventory, decided we needed a few more items, and Lisa showed me how to fill out the order forms. Thankfully, I was able to sit while doing that, but that was the only time all day.

"So how do you think it went?" I ask Candace.

She takes a drink from her cup and looks at me. "I think it went well. Mitch had a lot of business, and from what I could see, everyone seemed to be having a good time. I didn't hear any complaints, though that doesn't mean there weren't any."

Granny walks into the room and collapses onto

the sofa across from us. She grunts once she lands. "Well, they'd better not complain, that's all I've got to say."

"What's the matter, Granny, is your arthritis acting up again?"

She squirms in her seat like she's trying to get comfortable. "It sure is."

"You know, Granny, you don't have to do this." I can tell Candace is treading lightly here.

Granny's head jerks up. "I don't have to do anything except die and pay taxes. I want to do this for my grandson." She gives me a hard stare as though I have something to do with this discussion. I take another drink to avert her gaze.

"I know it, Granny," Candace soothes. "I'm only saying you don't *have* to do this. I feel badly that you're aching today, that's all."

Granny softens. "I'm sorry I bit at you, Candace. I guess Mitch isn't the only one who is touchy today."

Beneath that hard shell, I'm thinking there beats the heart of a gentle woman.

"It's all right. We're all a little tired and cranky," Candace says.

"How did you do today, Gwen?" Granny's question surprises me. She squirms a little more, obviously in pain.

"We had a lot of business today. No doubt I'll be making mochas and lattes in my sleep tonight."

Granny chuckles. "I guess you will. I don't know how people drink that stuff." Another grunt. Her nose wrinkles here, but I have to admit she looks kind of cute all crinkled up.

Right then the front door opens, and Mitch walks in. He's looking better than a large chocolate frappé with whipped topping. In my book, that says a lot.

"Well, there he is," Candace says. "How's my big brother doing?"

"Your big brother is tired," he says, shrugging off his winter wraps and boots and plopping down beside Granny on the sofa. I'm guessing he didn't notice the empty space beside me.

Mitch runs a weary hand through his hair. I wish he'd let me do that for him.

"You ready to eat?" Granny asks, though she doesn't look all that eager to get up.

"I am getting hungry," he admits.

"I'll be glad to get it for him," I say, hoping Granny won't resent my offer.

I'm surprised when she lifts a hopeful smile. "That would be nice, Gwen. Thank you." Granny kicks off her shoe and massages her big toe.

"You sure you don't mind?" Mitch asks, following me to the kitchen.

"I'm sure," I say over my shoulder, imagining that I'm Mrs. Windsor, and my husband has had a rough day on the slopes. I waltz into the kitchen. Now I'm no Martha Stewart, but I can take care of my man.

Once I pile his plate with meat loaf, potatoes, gravy, mixed vegetables and a dinner roll, I turn and plow right into him, knocking the plate to the floor. It shatters into tiny slivers across the ceramic tile and peas roll into every nook and cranny.

That's what I get for comparing myself to Martha Stewart.

I get on my knees, and start to scoop things into a pile. "I'm so sorry. I didn't know you were there. I have this terrible habit of not paying attention to things. I get my mind on other things or distracted or whatever—" I stop myself when I realize I'm babbling.

Mitch joins me on the floor. "It was my fault. I didn't mean to stand so close. It's just that you—"

I drop the peas I'm holding and look at him, waiting on his words. I have no idea what he's going to say, but something in his voice makes me think I want to hear this. We're on our knees, our faces mere inches apart. His gaze is fixed on me. I mean *really* fixed on me.

His face changes color right in front of me. Is

he… Yes, I believe he is—he's actually blushing here. How cute is that?

"It's just that you smelled like…well, what I mean to say is…your perfume, it kind of reminded me of Mom's perfume."

Did I hear what I think I heard? My imagination stops cold. He's telling me I smell like his mother? Quick, somebody sign him up for Romance 101. This is so not what I want to hear.

I stare back at him a little longer than I had intended, then I return to scooping peas in a pile. Once the debris is cleaned from the floor, for a fraction of a moment I consider giving him the rubbish to eat, but then I do the kind thing and gather a fresh plate of food.

I smell like his mother. If my mother heard that, she'd be calling Herbert Caudell.

We go back into the great room, and I announce that I'm going out for a while.

"Aren't you tired?" Candace looks at me with utter shock.

"Yes, but I need to pick up a few things from the store," I say, edging my way toward the stairs. When I imagined myself as Mrs. Windsor, I didn't mean Mitch's mother, for crying out loud.

This calls for an emergency trip to the store. I refuse to smell like his mother for one minute more.

Chapter Seven

It's hard to believe we're already gearing up for the weekend. The school group is coming today, so we have a busy day ahead of us. I open the front door.

"Are you going out now?" Granny asks.

"Well, that was the plan."

Granny makes a face. "Go ahead and do what you've got to do. One of these mornings I want to see if you can make a good omelet." With gnarled fingers balled into fists resting on her hip, she stares at me.

I gulp. "O-kay."

She snaps her head, turns on her heels and disappears into the kitchen before I can ask her what that's all about. She makes no bones about scrutinizing my talents—or lack thereof. No doubt about it, Granny wants to know if I'm capable of the cook's job before she releases the reins. Make no mistake, Granny's on a mission.

Heaven help us all.

We have an hour before opening so I'm in good shape time-wise when I step into the sunshine. The snow crunches beneath my boots, and the chill in the air makes my face tingle. I hate to admit it, but I'm almost getting used to this place. I walk toward the ski lift. Granny's ham-and-cheese omelet looked good this morning, but I've decided I've got to quit eating all her cooking, or I'll break the ski lift. Maybe when I cook for her, I'll make something healthy—something with wheat germ. Anything with wheat germ has to be healthy. No, I'd better not. Granny's all about taste, not health. I guess she figures she's lived this long without wheat germ, why start now? Come to think of it, that's my motto, too.

Tonight our first overnight guests are due to arrive for the weekend, which is kind of exciting. I know Mitch is getting anxious for overnight guests. Candace says it takes time for people to hear about the new businesses in the area.

Though I'm alone, I barely notice when the ski lift scoops me onboard. I'm training myself to keep looking forward and not actually think about the height. I've learned my lesson. We could have an avalanche or an earthquake beneath my feet, and it wouldn't matter. I refuse to look down.

Sunlight glistens off the snow ahead of me as I glide up the mountain. I take a deep breath and actually feel *total* peace. Well, okay, maybe not total peace. I do have a death grip on the bar in front of me, but at least I'm upright and breathing. Me. Riding up a mountain, in a ski lift. How weird is that?

I've been thinking of Mom and Dad lately. By the sounds of their recent phone call, though, they're having the time of their lives. I can't help feeling a little slighted. I mean, why can't they have that much fun when I'm with them? Not that I want to be cooped up in an RV with them.

I slide off the ski lift and make my way to the shop. Lisa will be here in a couple of hours. Things are always slow when we first open. I suppose that will change as word gets out about the resort.

Once I run through our supplies to make sure we have everything we need, I make myself a hot mocha. One of the perks of working here is I get all the drinks I want for free. Hey, that alone would have brought me here to work.

"Good morning!" Mitch walks through the door and shakes the snow from his jacket.

"It's snowing?"

"Yeah, coming down pretty good."

"I've been so busy getting things ready for the school group, I hadn't noticed. Want something to drink?"

He flashes one of those smiles that give me elf toes again. "That would be great."

"Americano or mocha?"

He looks surprised. "I'm an Americano man myself."

I raise my eyebrows. "I beg to differ. You ordered a mocha when you were with Monica the other day," I say, trying to act as though it doesn't matter to me one way or the other. I measure the espresso and water and start the machine.

He looks at me. "I did?"

"Yep, you did."

He shrugs. "I have more shots of espresso in my Americano. When I'm already jazzed, the last thing I need is more caffeine, you know?"

Well, this little bit of information certainly does not make me feel better. He was *jazzed* when he was with Monica. Jazzed as in battery running in full gear or jazzed as in nervous? I'm thinking I don't want to know this, so I set to work on his Americano.

"I don't want to get stuck in a rut, anyway. I'm into trying different things." I nod and give him the Americano. With my mocha in hand, I follow him to a nearby table. "Besides, sometimes I need something sweet."

We sit down. Something sweet? I bat my lashes a few times and put on my sweetest smile. "How do you feel about cashews?" I ask.

"Excuse me?"

"Never mind." Chocolate, cashews, whatever it takes. Can we talk long-term commitment here?

I'm picturing an open meadow, me, Hunky Boy on a blanket with the sun shining overhead and a picnic basket filled with chocolate between us. He lifts a chocolate-covered cashew to my lips and—

"Do you only drink mochas?" he asks.

And his words shatter my mirage into a hundred pieces. It takes me a moment to realize where I am, who I am, and what year this is. Though he's gorgeous, his timing stinks.

"Yeah. When I find something I like, I pretty much stick with it." I gather my courage. "So were you jazzed because of opening day or because of Monica Howell?" I tease, but now I feel kind of embarrassed that I've asked such a probing question.

"That's fair. The answer is both."

Great. The prom queen renders the quarterback speechless.

"Monica makes me nervous because I think she's digging for answers, trying to find out my next move, so she can one-up me."

I listen, feeling slightly guilty for enjoying his comments against Monica.

"I'm not sure I can trust her." He stares into his Americano then looks up at me. "But then she is helping me get the business off the ground, so I should be grateful." He smiles. "You know, you're easy to talk to."

I'm rather enjoying this little conversation. No, wait. Does he mean easy to talk to as in a girl who he could enjoy being with, or easy to talk to as in kid sister? I'm choosing to go with number one.

He stretches back, lifting the front legs of his chair off the floor. He glances at the clock on the wall. "We've still got a few minutes."

Stolen moments in time—together. The very idea makes me sigh out loud. When I hear myself, it startles me and I jerk. Not a little twitch, mind you. I'm talking a spasm that could set off an avalanche. The twitch sends my mocha from the table onto the floor.

Mitch's chair flops forward with a thud. I rush up to the counter and grab some paper towel to clean up the mess I've made. While I'm mopping up the floor I have visions of my senior prom, where I was crowned queen— well, almost.

I had walked up the stairs to the platform to

accept my crown. A friend down below waved at me. I lifted my hand to wave back and knocked the crown from Principal Hunt's hand. It went sailing through the crowd and landed on the floor. Unfortunately, the first person to pick it up was my dreaded rival—who had also run for prom queen.

Tense moments followed as we all waited with bated breath to see if she would bring the crown back to me. She did, but I think that's only because it was bent where someone had stepped on it. Probably her.

"You all right?"

Mitch's voice once again startles me back to the present, and I realize he's on the floor beside me, dabbing at spilled mocha with paper towels.

"I'm fine."

"We seem to do this a lot," he teases.

Thanks for the reminder. I lift a hesitant smile, and we continue to work in silence. We stand and walk the soiled towels over to the trash and plop them in.

"I guess I had better get out there," he says.

I've made such a mess of things. I look at him, not knowing what to say.

"It's no big deal, you know," he says as if reading my mind.

"Thanks, Mitch."

His eyes pin my heart in place for a full beat. "You're welcome." He turns and walks out the door. Only then do I feel my pulse kick in once again....

High school kids burst through the door of the coffee shop, laughing, bumping into tables, talking loud. They're tracking snow everywhere, and I don't mind. It's refreshing to see their happy faces. They're having a good time and it shows.

Lisa's making the drinks. All I have to do is collect the money. Talk about a great job.

"Hi, what can we get you?" I ask the first kid. I swallow hard when I see the influx of teens continue to enter the room. They keep coming and coming. It reminds me of those commercials where you see thirty people spill out of a compact car.

It takes some effort, but we finally get everyone taken care of, and the room settles down to a comfortable hum of voices. The fireplace crackles and sparks, spilling evergreen scents and warmth into the room. Outside the window, snow continues to fall from heavy gray clouds. I'm starting to wonder where Mitch has gone. He didn't make it to the inn for lunch. In fact, I haven't seen him since my fiasco this morning. He's probably decided to stay as far away from me as he can.

"Since the kids will be leaving in the next ten

minutes, do you mind if I go ski for a little while?" Lisa's question surprises me. I mean, she is still on the clock, but I guess that's between her and Mitch.

"It doesn't bother me," I say, meaning it. The kids are fairly quiet. I doubt anyone will order drinks before leaving anyway.

"Thanks." Lisa heads for the back room to get ready but returns a moment later.

"What's wrong?" I ask.

"I don't have enough money to rent skis, and I left mine at home," she says with obvious disappointment.

"Go down to the inn and tell Granny I said you could use my skis."

"I don't know." She bites her lower lip.

"Come on, Lisa, I don't mind at all. They really should be used."

"Don't you like to ski?"

I suddenly realize she's not aware of my aversion to skiing. "Sometimes, but let's just say it's not my favorite thing to do." I laugh.

"If you're sure you don't mind."

"I don't mind. Now go." I shoo her off with my hands and she heads out the door.

When the kids leave, I clean up the shop. I don't mind the solitude really—at first. My mind drifts to my friends back home. A sort of melancholy settles in, which is very unlike me. I don't do melancholy as a rule. Still, there it is. I decide tonight might be a good time to go visit Lauren and Garrett. I'll call first to make sure they don't already have plans. Hopefully, the weather will permit me to go somewhere.

The door swings open, and Lisa walks inside. She is covered with a layering of snow, her face is cherry red and her eyes are sparkling.

"What a rush!" she says, hobbling over to a table in her ski boots. I take the skis from her so she can pull her boots off.

"Did the skis work for you?" I call behind me.

"They were awesome!"

"Wish they'd work for me," I mutter under my breath.

Lisa tugs at her boots with a grunt. "Mitch joined me on a couple of runs. He is so cool."

Her comment sends a chill clear through me. He went skiing with her? Is she interested in him? Is he interested in her? A harmless ski down the mountain, that's all this is, right? There goes that green thing again. I might have to get rid of Guacamole. I think he's rubbing off on me. I have no claims on Mitch, so he can do what he wants.

"'Course, Monica came along and took him away."

And this is supposed to make me feel better?

"Wonder what she's doing here again," I say nonchalantly.

"Isn't it obvious?" Another grunt and Lisa pulls off the final ski boot. I walk over to her table and sit down.

"What do you mean?"

"I told you she's after him. She's been after him for years." She adjusts her socks and puts on her street boots. "I don't know her all that well, but from what I've heard, when Monica sets her sights on something, she gets what she wants."

"Well, she hasn't gotten him after all these years."

Something about the way she stares at me makes me a little uncomfortable. "True enough," she says. "Still, she's the patient sort. Keep in mind he's been abroad doing a little playing himself. His family isn't hurting for money, let me tell you."

I know that much, but I don't necessarily want to discuss it with her. Candace is one of my best friends, and I feel as though we're gossiping about her family. Come to think of it, that's exactly what's happening here.

"He's known as a player. Love 'em and leave 'em, they say, is his motto. In other words, he's not one to settle down. In fact, the scuttlebutt in town says this place won't last long." She shrugs. "He never sticks with a project. Gets bored too easily."

"People can change. Besides, he seems dedicated to this one," I defend, hoping I'm right. After all, I've put my life on hold for this opportunity. I don't want to head back to Arizona in a month or two, feeling every inch the failure.

"Maybe," she says with skepticism. "Hey, I was thinking you and I ought to get together sometime. You know, go shopping or something. Hang out together away from work."

I'm surprised by her offer, but it sounds good, all the same. "That would be great, Lisa. Thanks for offering." I don't want to blubber about feeling lonely, but her saying that makes me feel better.

"How about this weekend?"

I perk. "What do you have in mind?"

"Well, let's see, how about tomorrow night we go to a movie?"

Girls can do that without feeling all weird like guys sometimes do. "That would be fun." I try to hold my enthusiasm in check. She doesn't need to know that I have no life.

"Let's see, how about I come by and pick you up around five o'clock. That will give us time to grab a bite to eat, then head to the seven o'clock show."

"I'll be ready," I say, as Mitch walks into the room, all smiles. I'm feeling a little irritated with him, though I know I have no right. So what if he's been with Monica this afternoon?

"Hey, ladies. Too late to grab a coffee?" he asks me.

"I suppose I can squeeze in one more before closing shop," I tease.

"Well, I'm outta here," Lisa calls over her shoulder. We wave goodbye, and she closes the door behind her.

"Was it something I said?" Mitch asks.

"What?"

"She sure got out of here in a hurry."

I shrug. "I think she's tired from all that skiing today."

"I didn't see her skiing much. Mostly talking with the ski-lift operator. I was going to say something to her about that."

I look at him for a moment.

"What?"

"I don't know. She said she went skiing, and you and her skied a while."

He pulls off his coat and gloves. "I wouldn't call one time down the mountain 'a while,' but whatever." He scoots his chair back and plops his feet on the table. "I know I shouldn't do this. I'll clean off the table before I leave, I promise," he says with a grin.

I give him his Americano. "You're allowed. You're the boss."

"Thanks." He takes a drink from his cup.

"So do you think it went well with the kids today?" I ask.

"Yeah, I feel pretty good about it." He pulls open his lid and blows on the hot brew.

"Sorry if I got it too hot."

"No, I like it this way. It's fine." He replaces the lid.

"Um, Lisa said Monica dropped by again."

"Yeah. She's up to something, no doubt about it. If she comes in here asking questions, try to evade them. As I said before, I'm not sure I can trust her. She might truly be trying to help, but I don't know."

We talk a while longer then realize it's almost time for dinner. Mitch helps me clean up then we head down the mountain together on the ski lift.

He doesn't trust Monica, yet he's all aglow every time she's around. None of this makes sense. Now *I'm* beginning to wonder who to trust....

Chapter Eight

"I was on the phone with the family that's scheduled for tonight. They ran into some snow in their travels, and won't be here until tomorrow around noon," Granny announces when she steps into the great room.

I look at Mitch to see if he's upset. He seems all right with the news.

"Not much we can do about that," he says.

I'm beginning to love these evenings by the fire, sitting around just the way married couples do—well, Granny's with us, but still. The fireplace crackles in the distance, and I'm feeling a little giddy. I'm tired from the day, but I have some nervous energy. Maybe that second mocha put me over the edge.

"So how's the skiing going?" Mitch asks.

I've been trying to practice every day on the

bunny slope, but that's as far as I've gotten. At least he's noticed I'm making the effort. "It's going fine. I think I'm letting go of the Olympic gold, though."

He grins. "There are other worthwhile dreams in life."

Yeah, like you and me dressed in white, standing before a preacher perhaps? I smile.

He lifts his head and gazes out the window. "You know, it's pretty nice out there tonight. Little wind, dusk settling over the mountain. Full moon."

I have no idea what he's getting at, but that "full moon" business sends more shivers through me than the day my brother stuffed snow down the back of my shirt when we were kids. I look at Mitch, my heart in my throat.

"How about we ski the bunny slope?"

I stare at him as if I'm seeing double. "Let me get this straight. You want to ski with me on the *bunny* slope?"

He laughs. "Why not? Maybe I can give you a couple of pointers while we're out there." He sees my face and quickly adds, with hands up, "But no pressure. I promise." He crosses his heart with his finger.

I imagine myself on top of the mountain, spreading my arms wide, twirling, and singing, "The hills are alive…"

"It would be good for you to get some exercise," Granny says with her persuasive snap-to-it tone before sinking into a chair and sighing with pleasure.

Doggone it, I already made arrangements with Lauren.

"Uh-oh, I'm sensing some hesitation here," Mitch says.

"Well, the thing is I told Lauren I'd pop in tonight."

"No problem. We'll ski for maybe forty-five minutes, and then you can go. Better still, how about I go with you? I need to talk to Garrett about some business issues."

My gaze collides with Mitch's. Hard to imagine, but I'm so speechless I'm thinking my jaw has locked up on me here. Visions of me and Herbert Caudell sitting in his bookstore pouring over the latest novels are quickly fading. "Why not?"

"Great." He rises from the sofa. "I'll get on warmer clothes and meet you back down here in, say, fifteen minutes?"

"Sounds great." I head toward my room and resist the urge to take the stairs two by two. Actually, I could probably float to my room right about now, but instead I let my feet do the walking.

Once I'm ready, I see Mitch waiting for me. I

walk down the stairs with all the elegance of a prom queen—only this time, I throw only a smile, bat my lashes a few times and glide down the stairs with great elegance. Hey, this is my daydream; I can see it how I want to see it.

By the time I get downstairs, Mitch is smiling. Oh, this is feeling mighty fine. I've got a date—wait. Did I say date? Is that what this is? Let's see, we're skiing under the moonlight and going in a car together to visit some friends. I think this qualifies.

Party time!

Thankfully, Lisa returned my skis, so I grab them and we're good.

"I wasn't sure how you would adjust to being here since you don't enjoy the cold, but you seem to be handling it well," Mitch says, searching my face for some type of reaction.

I would go to the North Pole for you, Dream Boy. "I'm doing fine," I assure him. I glance away and sneak a look at my coat to make sure my beating heart isn't thumping noticeably against my jacket.

We ride the rope tow and finally land at the top of the bunny hill. I'm feeling a little silly that this experienced skier is doing this for me. He's probably bored to tears, but hey, if he's game, so am I.

At the top of the slope, Mitch pretty much tells

me everything that the guy at Dream Slopes told me, how to hold my legs, my arms, my body. It's like they think I can do three things at once. Have I mentioned I'm not good with multitasking? We manage to go down a few times, and I feel that my practice sessions are actually paying off. Within an hour, I'm sliding down the slope with Mitch by my side. And get this, I'm actually in control of my skis—well, sort of, anyway.

"Want to go down one last time?" he asks when we hit the bottom of the hill.

I glance heavenward. The moon is sailing beyond the treetops, the air is cold but not freezing, and when I look into his hazel eyes, I feel I have stepped into the wonder of an alpine forest. "Yeah," I say. I'm prom queen. I can do anything I want tonight.

We take the rope tow up once more. We stop at the top of the hill.

"Look at this place, Gwen," he says, looking around. "I mean, it's not the Alps, but isn't it magnificent?"

Of course we both know the view would be much better from the top of the mountain, but I'm good with pretending. "It is wonderful, Mitch." And it truly is. The views are beautiful from every angle.

"Beat you down," he says, darting off in a flash, kicking up white powder behind him.

"Hey! That's not fair!" I push off, trying, but failing, to catch up. The air is exhilarating against my skin—or maybe I just feel that way because I'm with Mitch. Racing down the slope, I get caught up in the thrill of the moment and turn my head to see the blazing colors splashed across the horizon. Somehow that motion gets me off balance, and I go sailing straight toward Mitch. I try to correct myself, but there's not enough time. He looks up a millisecond before I plow into him, and we spill upon the ground in a heap.

I don't know whether to laugh or cry. We're a tangled mess of legs, skis and poles. My head hurts, and my body feels slightly battered and bruised, but for some weird reason a giggle bubbles up in my throat, and I start laughing, and laughing, and laughing some more. Pretty soon Mitch joins me.

Our laughter rises on the wings of the wind as we sit in a muddled heap beneath a full moon.

"Well, well, well, what have we here?" Monica's voice startles us both.

The expression on her face makes me feel as though I've been caught doing something I shouldn't have been doing. Which, of course, is totally not true.

"Monica," Mitch says, pulling himself from our entanglement in no time and standing at attention.

"What are you doing here?" he asks, brushing the snow from his coat.

"You had asked for the names and prices of some of the vendors I use for the restaurant, and since I was in the area, I thought I would drop them by. Granny said you were out here." She lifts a manila folder that evidently has the information inside.

"Oh."

Hello? Anybody noticing that I'm struggling to get up?

"Obviously, I should have called first." She doesn't look happy.

I've never had strength in my arms. Picture quivering gelatin here. I'm hanging on to these doggone poles for all they're worth, but I don't have the strength to push myself up.

Mitch seems to waver with indecision. "No, I really appreciate that you've gone to the trouble—"

At this point, I stop struggling and stare at him. This is the man who says he doesn't trust Monica Howell? He talks about her one way to me, and treats her completely different. Maybe he's not even being honest with himself.

"So, do you want to look these over while I'm here, so I can answer any questions you might have?" she asks, making an obvious attempt to exclude me from this conversation.

Still trying to push myself up here. It's just not happening.

Mitch looks at me sitting sprawled out on the snow. "You need help getting up?"

Boy, nothing gets past this guy. "That would be great."

He extends his hand and lifts me up with no effort whatsoever.

"Thanks, Mitch." I brush myself off. I look over at Monica and the expression on her face— well, let me say merely that if this woman were a scorpion, I'd be dead right now.

Monica turns back to Mitch. "So, where can we go while you look through these?"

Mitch looks at me then back to Monica. "Actually, Gwen and I are going to visit some mutual friends. They're expecting us."

Monica stares daggers at me then lifts her chin. "Fine. Another time then," she quips. When she turns to go, I want to shout "Hooray," but the celebration sticks in my throat when Mitch stretches out his hand and grabs Monica by the arm.

"Hey, I'm sorry. I really do appreciate you going to the trouble to help me, Monica. I'll look them over tonight, and we can talk about them tomorrow, if that works for you—or better still, call me tomorrow, and we'll arrange a time to go over them together," he says, as though he can't wait to meet her again.

Her chin lifts along with the corners of her mouth when she looks my way. Then she gazes back at Mitch, fully armed with all her feminine charm. "I'll do that." Her expression says far more than her spoken words.

I watch after her and feel a hollow victory. I should feel ashamed for what I'm thinking, because I want to kick Mitch in the shins! First he tells me he doesn't trust her, the next thing he does is practically make a date with her right in front of me. The more I think about it, the madder I get.

"You know, I think I'll drive myself over to Lauren's. I may want to come home sooner than you." I feel a slight amount of pleasure when I see the surprise on his face.

"That's not a problem. I can leave when you do."

"No, I think it would be best to drive separately." I turn and head toward the house before he has a chance to comment.

I hear his quick breaths behind me as he rushes to catch up. "Gwen, wait. Have I made you angry for some reason?"

For some reason? *For some reason?* He's kidding, right? That was just wrong. "No, I'm not angry." All right, so maybe I am angry, but it's not something I can talk about now. Besides, the fact that I said that through clenched teeth should give him a clue.

He grabs my arm—the same as he grabbed Monica's—and turns me to face him. Both of his hands are holding me in place now. "Gwen, what's wrong?"

The sound of his voice, and the look on his face make me weak in the knees. Mitch steps closer to me, causing a gasp to catch in my throat. I see his gaze travel from my eyes to my lips. I would gulp right about now if I had any air left in my lungs. His head dips toward me….

"Somebody wants you on the phone, Mitch," Granny calls from the back door.

"I'll be right there, Granny," he says, his gaze never leaving my face. "Don't go without me, Gwen." The deep emotion in his voice turns my insides to butter. My heart couldn't beat any faster if I were being chased by a wolf.

I can only hope that's not what's happening here.

Chapter Nine

After refreshing my makeup, I come down the stairs with high expectations of my upcoming time with Mitch as we go to Lauren and Garrett's together. I don't know what's happening between us, but it has definite possibilities. It amazes me, because I can't imagine a guy like him looking twice at someone like me. Maybe it's the cold mountain air, in which case, he could never go to Arizona with me.

"You going out?" Granny asks, already dressed in her pajamas, robe and slippers. Her appearance stuns me a little. I've never seen her without her, um, teeth. Didn't know she could take them out, as a matter of fact. I try not to stare. She looks a little vulnerable, softer somehow. Doesn't have quite the usual bite to her appearance—did I really just think that?

"Yeah, I—we were going to go visit Lauren and Garrett Cantrell."

"That's Candace's college friend, too, isn't it?" Granny settles onto the sofa.

I nod.

"Candace tells me the three of you were inseparable in college."

I smile with the remembrance. "That we were."

Granny pins me with a stare as though she's trying to see into my soul or something. The woman takes life way too seriously.

"Then there's Mitch. Wouldn't know a good friend if he had one." She looks toward the window. "He's made some wrong choices, that one. Had his heart broken a time or two." She says it as though she's talking to someone across the room, then she turns to me again. "But it won't happen again, if I have anything to say about it." Her jaw clenches.

I have no idea what she's talking about. I am curious about the broken heart thing, but I figure Mitch will tell me one day if we ever get that close. Granny's still watching me, so I dig through my purse for some gum. That always makes me feel better. I find a stick, unwrap it and plop it in my mouth. I look up to her with a smile. I would offer her some, but well, there's that whole teeth issue.

Mitch walks into the room wearing a serious

expression. Good grief, these people need to lighten up.

"Granny, I've got to go out. I'll be back later."

I start to rise, when he turns to me.

"Sorry, Gwen, you'll have to go to Lauren's without me."

"Is everything all right, Mitch?"

"Everything is fine," he says and walks away.

No explanation, nothing. Mitch only tells me to go on alone. "I'm stupid for letting it get me down," I say out loud as I pull into Lauren's parking lot.

Clicking off the engine, I make my way to their front door, determined to not let this whole episode get the better of me. I've always sailed through life, allowing very few people to ruin a perfectly good day. I figure if I have a bad day, it's my own fault. No one can hurt me if I don't let them, right?

"Hey, Gwen, come on in!" Lauren is standing, smiling at the front door. I feel better already.

"Hi, Gwen," Garrett says when we enter the great room.

"Take a seat on the sofa. I'll get us some hot tea—is that all right?"

"Sure, Lauren. Thanks."

"You sit down with Gwen, I'll get it for you,"

Molly says when she and Macy enter the room. They are Garrett's teenage daughters from his first marriage. Their mother died in a car accident.

"Macy and Molly, good to see you girls," I say, rising to give them a hug. I love these girls. So well-behaved and friendly.

"You want some, Dad?" Molly asks.

"Sure. Bring it in the den, will you?" Garrett rises from his chair and turns to me. "I'm afraid I have some work to do. Is Mitch coming?"

"Um, no. Something came up," I explain. I have no idea what, of course, but I don't know what else to say.

Lauren and Garrett both look surprised.

"That's too bad. Maybe another time." He looks at Lauren. "Well, I'll leave you two alone to visit."

Once he leaves the room, Lauren turns to me on the sofa. "Time to spill your guts. What's going on with you and Mitch?"

I brush a crumb from my jacket. "I don't know what you're talking about."

"Oh, come on, Gwen. Candace told me she could see some chemistry between you two."

My head jerks up. "She did?" That makes me too happy for words.

Lauren looks pleased for telling me the good news. "Yes, she did. And we both know that Candace knows her brother well."

I feel a sudden spurt of hope. Bring on the balloons.

She grins and leans in toward me. "So? Anything going on?"

"No, not really. I mean, I don't know for sure, but well, we had a nice time this evening."

"Let's hear it."

I stop long enough for Macy and Molly to hand us our teacups, talk a moment about school, then leave the room.

I then tell Lauren about the moonlit skiing and how close we were when Granny called him in for a telephone call, then how things seemed to change after that.

"Hmm, that is interesting. Something must have happened."

"Definitely, I just don't know what."

Lauren takes a sip of tea. "Could be any number of things."

"You know, you're right. I was thinking he didn't want to come with me, but it's probably something else entirely."

"Absolutely. He wouldn't have been so 'friendly' earlier, Gwen, if he wasn't interested in you." She hesitates a minute. "I'm surprised in you. You're always the one to see the bright spot in things. It's not like you to think the worst."

I sigh. "When it comes to my heart, it's a little harder to believe the best, you know?"

Lauren smiles softly. "Yeah, I guess it is at that."

"So, how is married life?" I pick up my tea and stir it a couple of times to cool it off before taking a drink.

"It's great, Gwen." She whispers, "Garrett is everything I have ever dreamed of in a husband."

The comment warms me. I'm so happy for Lauren. "God was watching out for you, Lauren."

She looks up and smiles again. "He really was. You know, Gwen, He's watching out for you, too."

I nod. "You think He remembers that whole biological clock thing?"

Lauren laughs. "Still worried about your mom forcing you to marry Herbert?"

I make a face. "The thought does cross my mind from time to time."

"This is the twenty-first century, Gwen. Parents don't force their children into prearranged marriages anymore."

"You obviously underestimate my mother."

We both laugh.

"Herbert would probably show up at the wedding in white polyester pants," I say, giggling.

"And white patent-leather shoes!" Lauren teases.

I place my tea in the coaster and fall back against the sofa. "Oh, don't say that!"

"Poor Herbert," Lauren says.

"I know. I really shouldn't tease that way. He's a good guy, just not my type. He'll make some woman a fine husband one day—well, if you're into polyester, anyway." I press my lips together so I'll behave myself.

We talk a little while about how close Lauren is getting to Macy and Molly and how much she loves living in Bliss Village.

She smiles. "And you know, I never in a million years thought I'd get to have you as a neighbor."

I perk once again. "I know. Isn't this great? I have to say I love it here, too."

"It doesn't hurt to work around a hottie like Mitch Windsor, either, huh?"

I feign ignorance. "Merely trying to be a good employee." I look at the clock. It's close to ten. "Goodness, I've stayed long enough. I need to get going."

"You don't have to rush off."

I rise from the sofa. "No, I really need to go. I'd like to go to church on Sunday. Can you recommend any place nearby?"

"How about visiting our church?"

"That would be great," I say, feeling better about going where I know someone.

"Let me write the directions down for you," Lauren says, making her way to a desk in the room. She pulls out a tablet of paper and a pen. After diagramming the directions, she hands the paper to me. "I've added my cell phone number in case you get lost."

Directions aren't my strong suit, and she must see the fear on my face.

"Don't worry. It's easy to find from your place," she says, as if I live at the resort with Mitch. Oh, wait. I do. Well, not exactly "with" Mitch, but there at the property anyway.

"Great." I stuff the paper in my purse. "Thanks, Lauren."

"You're welcome. I wrote the service times down, so you can decide which service you want to attend. Our family goes to the second service."

"Great, I'll plan to come then."

We say our goodbyes, and I get in my car to head back to the B and B. I have to admit I'm feeling much better about things after visiting with Lauren. She and Candace always make me feel better. I could never have gotten through college without their support. Now it looks as though I'm going to depend on them through life, as well.

I turn on my Barry Manilow CD, and pull up to a traffic light on a one-way street. A love song fills the air and lightens my heart. I turn to the car next to me and have to mentally shake myself when I see the profile of the man in the passenger's seat. He resembles Mitch. I refocus. Wait. It *is* Mitch! But who's the driver? I crane my neck to see. The driver turns to talk to the passenger. She says something and they both look over at me. My heart sinks. The driver is smiling and waving.

It's Monica Howell.

Somehow I manage to get through the next day without talking to Mitch.

I take one last look at myself in the mirror. Rust-colored sweater, khakis, matching hoop earrings and bracelet and cute tan boots complete my outfit. I'm looking forward to going to the movies with Lisa. I need to get away from Windsor Mountain for a while. I've allowed my emotions to run rampant concerning Mitch Windsor, and I need to get a grip. I've been watching too many romance movies, I think. Hmm, I wonder what movie we're seeing tonight. Hopefully, not a romance.

Mitch should still be out on the mountain, so hopefully, I won't run into him before I leave for the movies. Guacamole trots along the floor behind me. "You behave yourself, young man," I say before I step through the door, leaving him behind.

I'm feeling pretty chipper, despite everything. I practically gallop down the stairs and stop in front of the door as it opens.

Mitch steps inside.

"Wow, you look great," Mitch says, looking up at me.

I can feel the heat in my face. "Thanks."

"Going somewhere?"

"Yeah, to a movie."

"Alone?" He pins me with his stare. Suddenly, I don't want to fill him in on all the details. After all, he didn't give me any last night.

I smile brightly. "Nope." I swish past him. "Have a great evening," I say happily as I slip through the door, hopefully, leaving him gaping behind me.

Lisa and I have a great time. We're really bonding, and I think she could become a good friend. I've decided she doesn't have an interest in Mitch, other than as a friend.

We're headed out of the theater and walking to our cars. Since the movie was later than expected, we decided to drive separately.

"So what do you think Mitch will do to keep ahead of Monica?"

Her question seems to come out of nowhere, but I guess that's how women think most of the time anyway. "I have no idea. Other than he thinks they offer two different things to people. Her place has more of a big feel to it, he says. He's hoping his place offers a cozy, homey feeling and will attract more families, couples, that kind of thing."

"Oh, that makes sense."

I dig in my purse for my keys.

"Does he have any special plans for discounts, that sort of thing?"

"Do you think Mitch tells me everything or something?" I ask with a laugh.

"Well, you two do seem kind of chummy," she teases.

"Trust me, we're not that chummy."

"Oh, that's too bad."

I turn to her and see her grinning. "I think I'll survive." The jury's still out on that one.

We walk along in silence. A few people wander by on the way to their cars. My keys clink together as they dangle from my fingers. We arrive at our cars, which are parked next to one another.

"I had a great time, Lisa. Thanks for thinking of this."

"I did, too. We'll do it again soon. See you Monday," she says before ducking into her car.

I make my way home and pull into the parking lot of the B and B. I see an unfamiliar car, so I'm figuring the guests finally arrived. Mitch will be happy. The place looks dark. I try to be quiet when I step inside.

I slip open the door and hear some voices in the kitchen. Taking off my jacket, I step toward the kitchen. I think the voices belong to Granny and Mitch, so I want to tell them good-night, so they don't think me rude. As I'm about to round the corner, their conversation stops me.

"Well, Mitch, you'd better be careful," Granny's voice warns. "She might think you're interested in her, and then you'll get yourself in a real pickle."

"I think she knows we're only friends, Granny. She's not my type. She should get that by now."

The knots in my stomach could win a Girl Scout award. I swallow hard and turn toward my room. I know Mitch and I don't have anything going really, but last night he did sort of give me the idea he might be interested. I knew better. I should have listened to my mind instead of my heart. He couldn't possibly be interested in someone like me. I was an idiot for thinking otherwise.

When my right foot hits the bottom stair, a piercing shriek bounces off the walls. It sends chills straight through me.

Mitch comes running through the room, with Granny walking hesitantly behind him.

"Was that you?" he asks, his eyes wide.

I shake my head and point toward a room upstairs.

He rushes past me, up the stairs to the opening door of a guest room.

"There's a—a—big lizard or something in my closet," the woman says, practically on the verge of hysteria.

Guacamole! I run up the stairs, and Mitch turns to me. I'm not liking the look on his face right about now.

We ease into the couple's room. The woman is standing up in the middle of the bed, pacing a few steps back and forth, eyes wide, face flushed, her fists pressed hard against her lips. The man is trying to back Guacamole in a corner. Not a good thing.

"Sir, you'd better let me help you," I warn.

The man looks at me with surprise. I step past him. My worst fears are confirmed. Guacamole is alert and standing at attention. His tail swishing back and forth—as though *he* has a reason to be agitated.

"Guacamole, what are you doing in here?" I ask. Not that I expect him to answer, but it seems like the thing to say anyway.

I ease him past the gaping couple, offering Guacamole a sliver of carrot from my pocket—who knows how long it's been there. I haven't been on a diet since eighth grade. I grovel my apology to the couple. I don't even glance up at Mitch. His face was too red when I saw him before, and I don't want him to explode.

I hear Mitch explaining to the couple about Guacamole, and he assures them it won't happen again. I ease Guacamole into my room and look up right before I close the door. Mitch is standing close at hand.

"We'll talk tomorrow," he says. The look on his face tells me this weekend isn't going to get any better.

Chapter Ten

"I have no idea how you're getting out of here, Guacamole, but you can be sure it's not going to happen today, mister." I yank the door of my room closed behind me, assuring that snoopy iguana stays put on the Lord's day. I can't imagine why Guacamole keeps wandering out anyway. He hates the cold, and it's definitely colder in the open hallways than in our room with his special lighting.

Oh, well, I'm going to church, and with the door firmly shut, I don't need to worry about him.

I slip down the stairs, my hand running along the freshly polished banister. Shame on me for messing up the shine, but it feels so nice. Kaci, the housekeeper, came last night rather than morning. Wonder if she's accidentally letting Guacamole out? Maybe I should talk to Mitch about it. I notice Mitch gives her flexible hours to accommodate her college load. He's pretty under-standing with people, I'll give him that. Not that I want to think about him right now.

Once my coat and hat are on, I step outside. Tiny flakes are falling from the sky. The whole area has a storybook charm to it.

One glance in the parking lot tells me that the inn guests have already gone. I'm afraid Guaca-mole has chased them off. Mitch will be doing the same thing to me soon.

My brother *so* owes me for bringing this iguana into my life.

I brush the light snow from my windshield and start up my car engine. The cold makes me shiver. I snuggle deeper into my coat. After I turn up the heater, I head onto the road.

By the time I reach Lauren and Garrett's church, I'm feeling a little nervous and wanting to back out. But of course that's silly. I'm a grown woman. I can take on the challenge of a new setting, new people, new experiences, right? I mean, that's the very reason I came to Bliss Village in the first place.

"Gwen, you made it!" Lauren rushes over and hugs me the minute I walk through the doors.

"Did you think I wouldn't come?" I laugh. She knows me well.

Lauren lifts a teasing grin. "Well, the thought

did occur to me." She grabs my hand and drags me with her. "I have some people I want you to meet." She introduces me to some of her friends and then whisks me off to the sanctuary. "I have to get to choir, but I'll leave my Bible and purse here with you. Garrett and I will join up with you after choir, will that work?"

"Sure, that's great," I say, smiling, all the while wishing I didn't have to sit alone. Be brave. Be brave. I watch Lauren flitter off down the gray-carpeted aisle and think how thankful I am to have her and Candace for friends.

"Mind if I sit here?"

I turn to the deep voice beside me, and my heart does a back flip.

"Hi, Mitch," I say, sliding Lauren and Garrett's Bibles over a couple of seats, and scooting to the right to make room for him.

He turns those hazel eyes to me. He is mere inches from my face. "I didn't know you were coming here today."

I wanted to say, "Well, I don't tell you everything," but his breath is all spearminty and warm against my skin, and I forget what he said.

He keeps looking at me. "Gwen?"

Don't bother me. I'm picking up the scent of your cologne. I want one more whiff. Still staring. Just a tiny whiff. "Yes."

"I said I didn't know you were coming here today."

"I didn't know you attended here," I say, truthfully.

"Really? I figured Lauren told you."

I shake my head. "Well, it's not as though we talk about you," I blurt. Why did I say that? We have actually discussed him a little. Would you believe, a lot? Not that I want him to know that. The look on his face makes me wish I'd kept my mouth shut.

He clasps his fingers together and looks at them. "Oh, sure, I know, I thought she might have mentioned—"

"Hey, I'm sorry, Mitch. I didn't mean it to sound quite that way."

He looks up at me. "You didn't?"

Boy, something in the way he says that makes my knees buckle. Hard to do when you're in a sitting position, believe me.

What am I thinking? This is the man who ditched me for Monica Howell. How can I let him back into my good graces so easily? I turn away. I will not be won so easily. I want to ask him about it, but the music has started, and this isn't the time. I simply smile at him and turn my attention toward the worship service. I admit it's hard to keep focused with him sitting close beside me.

Not to mention the fact I'm confused by everything.

Before long, though, I'm lost in the music, in worship, in the service. Lauren and Garrett soon join us and the pastor speaks on Psalm 139.

It amazes me that the Lord can know me so intimately, and I haven't even figured out who I am myself yet. I want to think on that some more, study that chapter. I feel there's something in that for me.

"Hey, you ready to go?" Lauren is tugging at my sleeve, smiling.

"Oh, yeah. Sorry."

"Great message, huh?" Lauren says just behind me as we make our way from our chairs.

"Yes, it was. I really enjoyed myself this morning. I like your church a lot, Lauren. Thanks for inviting me."

"I'm glad you came." She nudges my back and whispers, "It's obvious someone else is glad you came, too." I look to her and smile. She tips her head toward Mitch, who is walking in front of us with Garrett. We edge our way out of the sanctuary, and the guys turn to us.

Lauren walks over to whisper something to Garrett who smiles and nods in response.

"Hey, how about you two join us for lunch?" Lauren is all smiles. I'm mortified. I haven't had a chance to tell her about Mitch and Monica.

"That would be great," I hear Mitch say. "That is, if Gwen isn't sick of seeing me. After all, she works and lives with me."

My head jerks toward him. Lauren and Garrett smother a chuckle.

Mitch holds up his hands. "Oh, I didn't mean lives with me, exactly, I meant—"

Now, here's the best part. His face actually turns two shades of red.

"Don't worry about it, dude," Garrett says, patting Mitch on the back. "We know what you meant."

Doggone it. I wanted to hear him get out of that one. We all start for the door when Mitch grabs my arm. "No sense in both of us driving out there. You want to ride with me?"

Before I can answer, I see Lauren turn to me. She smiles and gives me a discrete nod, as though I can't make the decision myself. Excuse me, but this one is a no-brainer. It's true that I'm a little mad at him over that whole Monica thing, but I'm not stupid.

"I guess that's all right," I say, like it's no big deal, which, of course, it is.

A strong leather scent greets me as I climb into his silver luxury car. "Is this new?" I ask.

"No, I've had it a couple of years."

I'm impressed that he keeps his car so nice and shiny. That's a nice quality in a man. It tells me that he'll help pick up things around the house when he's married one day. Wait a minute. It could mean that he's a neat freak. I give him a sideways glance. Hair perfectly in place. That's it. He's a neat freak. Probably even color-codes his underwear. Probably has control issues. Okay, now he's scaring me.

"Listen, Gwen, about Friday night—"

Oh, I'm glad he pulled me out of that, but do I want to hear about Friday night?

"I know I left suddenly, and I feel I owe you an explanation."

"No, you don't, Mitch." What am I saying here? Of course he owes me an explanation.

"Well, I want to give you one anyway."

Um, if you insist.

"I got a call—" I notice he hesitates here "—from Monica on her cell phone. She was all distressed about a near-accident and asked me to come over." He sighs. "I know she plays her little games, but I wasn't sure if she was in trouble, so I went over. No matter how she drives me crazy, we do have a past. Been friends forever, and I care about her."

Over-sharing here. I don't like that part. Happy attitude waning. He can stop now.

"So I felt I needed to go check. Of course, it ended up being nothing, and she wanted to grab a coffee. I can't afford to make her mad right now while she's helping me."

Silence. That's it? Are you sure you don't have something to add to this story?

"Anyway, I'm sorry we didn't go to Lauren and Garrett's together. And I'm glad we're getting this chance today." His grin lifts from his mouth to his eyes.

And this is supposed to make it all better? I think not. "So do you always do that?"

His grin teeters a smidge. "Do what?"

"Run to Monica at her every call?" I know this is none of my business, but he's taking away my good mood, and that's just wrong.

I don't miss the fact that his body stiffens. He places both hands tight on the steering wheel. I might have popped one of his balloons. I'm feeling a little justified.

"If my friends need me, I'm there for them." His mouth thins into a taut line. I could time his pulse right now by watching that vein thump in his neck.

"I see. No matter if you have plans or not."

"Look, Gwen, I know we sort of had plans, but nothing was concrete, and it's not like we had a date or anything."

Oh, sure, rub it in my face. I straighten my back and plant my feet firmly on the floor. "I understand."

"The more you get to know me, the more you'll see that I don't like to let people down."

"Oh?" Could have fooled me.

"What do you mean, 'oh'?"

"Nothing."

"Yes, you did. You meant something by that 'oh.' If there's one thing I can't stand, it's when people act as though they don't mean anything when they know good and well they mean something."

He can't stand? Did he say he "can't stand"? "I'm sorry that you have a problem with my saying 'oh,' Mitch, but there it is." I say this in a chipper voice but we both know that my perky self has long since left. As in pulled up stakes and not coming back any time soon.

He drives into the Cantrells' parking lot, clicks off the engine and turns to me. "Are you saying I let you down? I invited myself to go along with you, if I remember right. You didn't ask me to go, remember? So I didn't figure it was any big deal."

"You're right. It wasn't any big deal," I say, promptly getting out of the car and slamming the car door behind me. I practically run into the house, mumble to Lauren that I need to go to the bathroom and rush past her. I have no idea why I'm acting so emotional over this. I think it's because, number one, he raised his voice to me, and, number two, we were having our first fight over *Monica Howell.*

Once inside the bathroom, I lock the door and stand in front of the sink a moment to catch my breath. He's my boss. Nothing more. I shouldn't be having this conversation with him. It's all stupid. I have no claims on this man. He sees himself as my friend, and now I've acted like a jealous girlfriend. If that doesn't make him run, nothing will.

A soft knock on the door. "Gwen, what's going on? Are you all right?" Lauren whispers.

I swallow. "Yes, I'm fine." I open the door.

Lauren pushes me back inside and closes the door behind us. "What is it?"

"Nothing."

"Come on, something's wrong."

I quickly fill her in on the highlights of our argument and what happened Friday night.

"Oh." She chews on her lower lip.

"Last time I said 'oh,' it started a fight."

She looks up at me, and we both start to laugh.

Another knock on the door. "Everything all right in there?" Garrett wants to know.

Lauren covers a giggle with her hand then says, "Yes, honey, we're fine. We'll be right out."

"I think those two are up to something," we hear him say as he edges farther down the hallway.

Lauren puts her hand on my arm. "You're beginning to care about him, aren't you, Gwen?" She searches my face. "I mean, really care about him."

I look her straight in the eyes. I've been fooling myself up to this point. I mean, I know I've been attracted to Mitch from the get-go, but caring about him, in a special way? I hadn't really analyzed that one. "I might be."

Her face shows concern. "Tread easy. I don't want you to get into the same kind of mess I was in with Jeff," she says, referring to her ex-fiancé, who dumped her for another woman. "We both love Candace, and we know she and her brother are close, but we also know he has a past."

I'm trying very hard to forget that part.

"He seems to be a great guy, but I don't want him to hurt you."

I smile. "I don't want him to, either."

"You sure you want to keep working there?"

"What, do you think I'm a quitter?" I act all aghast, and Lauren smiles. "No, I can stick it out. I need to do this. For me."

"I understand," Lauren says before giving me a quick hug. "Now, we'd better get out there, or we'll be eating burned steaks."

I glance once more at myself in the mirror and straighten my hair.

"You look wonderful," Lauren says.

We walk down the hall and into the great room. Garrett looks from Lauren to me, back to Lauren. Mitch looks only at me.

"Well, I see you got yourselves some iced tea," Lauren says to Garrett. "I'll get some for Gwen and me."

"Already did," Garrett says with a teasing glint in his eye. He points to the two glasses of tea on a nearby stand.

"Thanks. I'd better check on the steaks. Be right back," she says to me.

I look for a place to sit and there's a space beside Garrett on the sofa or beside Mitch on the other sofa.

"I won't bite. I promise," Mitch says, and I hear a sort of apology in his tone.

The thump of my heart matches the first day I went up the ski lift, and I try to pick up my glass of tea without causing the ice cubes to bounce around too much from my shaking hand.

"So Mitch tells me you're doing a good job at the coffee shop," Garrett says.

I shrug. "It's a fun job. I'm meeting a lot of nice people."

"She works well with Lisa Jamison, too."

Garrett smiles. "Do you miss teaching?"

I don't know why but I look at Mitch and what

I see of his expression surprises me. It's as if he's not sure he wants me to answer that question.

"Yeah, I miss the students. But this is good for me. I needed a break. I think I was getting burnt out. This job opportunity came at a good time."

Lauren comes into the room and announces lunch. The girls are gone to their friends' houses, so it's only the four of us. We enjoy a nice meal and fellowship together. Once the table is cleared, we retreat back into the great room with our cups of coffee in hand. Garrett says something to Mitch and he turns to leave. "I'll be right back," Mitch says to me. "I have to get something out of the car."

I guess he thought he had to tell me what he was doing so I wouldn't think he was going to meet Monica again.

Pretty soon he steps back into the room, and he's holding a guitar case. He places it on the floor and pulls out a beautiful acoustic guitar.

"Is that your guitar?" I ask, amazed that he hasn't mentioned this before now.

"Yep." He strums the strings to tune it. "Garrett, you told me to bring this in. What do you want to sing?"

"Oh, I love this," Lauren says. "I'm glad you thought of this, Garrett." She snuggles up next to him on the sofa, and I'm suddenly feeling lonely.

Mitch walks over to the sofa beside me, and he starts singing a worship song that is new to me. Lauren and Garrett join in. I close my eyes to concentrate on the words they are singing. Their voices blend perfectly. I feel a bit like an outsider, but I don't dwell on that. I'm lost in the beauty of their offering.

One song leads to another. Before we know it, we've gone through five or six tunes, and we're having a wonderful time.

"Would you like to play?" Mitch asks me.

"Oh, no, I wouldn't know how," I say, feeling giddy at the thought.

"I can help you." He scoots closer to me on the sofa. I glance up at Lauren and she smiles. He places the strap of the guitar around my shoulders. He tries to put my fingers on the strings, but we're having trouble.

I start to giggle. "Sorry, I'm not very flexible."

"Why don't you stand up? I can help you better that way."

I stand, and he comes over to the left of me. He puts his hand on my hand, stretching my fingers into position on the strings. "You put this finger here, and this one here, and I'll start you on an easy tune."

"You mean right here?" I ask, pushing my finger against the string. He turns to me and our faces are so close, I can feel the brush of his breath on my cheek. He looks into my eyes, and I'm sure I'm going to melt into a puddle on the floor.

"Yeah, right there," he says, his gaze never leaving my face. For the moment, I'm lost in his eyes, the touch of his fingers, his breath on my cheek—until Nocchi, Lauren's cross-eyed Shih Tzu, barks at a bird she's watching through the window, bringing us both back to our senses.

Embarrassed, I quickly look at Lauren and Garrett, who are both smiling. They turn away when they see me and busy themselves.

Well, this is awkward.

"I don't think I can do this right now," I say, taking the guitar from my shoulders. "I'd rather hear you play anyway."

"Would anyone like some popcorn?" Lauren asks, already rising.

"Actually, I think we've kept you long enough, maybe we'd better get going," Mitch says.

"You don't have to rush off," Garrett interjects.

"No, it's fine. I have some things to do this afternoon," I say, though I can't think of them right now. I want to leave this place, this moment, and sort through it all in the privacy of my room.

Mitch and I thank the Cantrells for a wonderful time, and we ride back to my car at the church in silence.

"Listen, Gwen, I'm not sure what happened back there, but—"

"What do you mean? Nothing happened." I play naive—as if I haven't a clue what he's talking about. Maybe I should let him talk, tell me how much he's in love with Monica, and he didn't mean anything by what happened, but I can't.

For now I want to revel in what might have been....

Chapter Eleven

"We might as well get comfortable while Mitch makes his phone call," Granny says, easing onto the thick brown sofa cushion in the great room. She pushes the plump rust-colored pillows aside to make room for her knitting basket.

I hear Mitch punch the numbers on the phone and try not to think about who will answer on the other end of the line. Pine logs crackle and sputter as the flames dance about in the hearth. A spicy perfume fills the air. I'm mesmerized by the flames until Granny stirs, and I see her pull out some knitting needles and yarn.

"I didn't know you knew how to do that."

She looks up in surprise. "Oh, my, I've been knitting for probably thirty to thirty-five years now."

I get up from my chair, walk over and sit beside her on the sofa. "What are you making?"

She looks up and smiles. "A baby blanket. My friend's granddaughter is having a baby in a couple of months. They already know she's a girl."

I nod, taking in the muted pastels of the baby-soft yarn. "She'll love it."

"Do you knit?"

I shake my head. "I tried crocheting once, but I can't seem to sit still long enough." I laugh.

Granny stares at me a moment, and I see a slight crinkle at the edge of her eyes. "I was the same way when I was your age," she says. "That's why I didn't knit until later."

I glance toward the window and see a light sprinkling of snow drifting on the breeze. Heavy boots scuffle toward the room entrance, and I turn to see Mitch standing there.

"Did you take care of things?" Granny asks.

"Yes, as a matter of fact, I did." A wide grin stretches across his face as though he and Granny share a secret. He looks at me.

"What?"

"Well, I didn't know if you would be up for this, but you had mentioned to me once that it would be a good idea to offer sleigh rides to our guests, and I wanted to check out the possibility."

I'm liking the sounds of this.

"A friend of mine is bringing his rig—his sleigh

and team of horses—here in a few minutes to let me try it out. Do you want to go?"

It's all I can do not throw my arms around him. "Sure, that would be great," I say with a calm enthusiasm—although my insides are screaming, "Are you kidding me? I'm *so* there!"

Mitch and Granny exchange another glance, and I can't help but wonder what they're up to. So far they've said nothing more about Guacamole, so I'm hoping we're past that crisis. Could it be that Granny is warming up to me? She's acted dead set against me from the start, but lately, she's been nicer. She does pump me with a million questions. I have to wonder if she's a frustrated reporter. Still, I like her.

The doorbell rings.

Mitch looks at me and grins. "That must be him."

I reach into the closet and lift my thick woolen coat from the hanger. I stuff my arms into the sleeves and quickly button up. Rubbing the cashmere scarf between my fingers fills me with nostalgia as I remember the Christmas Mom and Dad bought it for me. Mom would keel over right about now if she knew I was going on a sleigh ride under a moonlit sky with a handsome man. She'd have the wedding invitations ordered, addressed and stamped and be on her way to the post office before we could return from our ride.

Mitch steps into the hallway. "You ready to go?"

"I'm ready."

He reaches for my hand, though I have no idea why, and leads me out the door. "Be back soon, Granny," he calls over his shoulder.

"You kids have a good time," Granny yells back.

Mitch waves goodbye to his friend, who has dropped off the team and is now driving away in Mitch's car.

"You get the horses and he gets your car?" I ask as Mitch helps me into the sleigh.

He chuckles. "That's pretty much it. Though I think I'm getting the better deal." His eyes hold mine and suddenly I'm caught up in a fairy tale.

The moon glows upon the glistening snow, offering a soft light along our path. All I can hear are the muffled sounds of the horses' hooves clip-clopping along the isolated path. There's a slight breeze, and though it is chilly, it's not freezing.

Snow-laden pines stand in the distance across rough mountain slopes and backwoods terrain.

"There are some blankets, if you get too cold." Mitch nods toward the backseat.

I pull a couple of them from the back and lift them onto the seat, spreading them carefully across my legs.

"You want some?"

"I'm fine for now," he says. "So what do you think?"

"Mitch, it is gorgeous." I really mean that.

"There's something magical about a night like this," he says, almost in a whisper.

Magical. Yes, that's what it is. Magical. Tonight I'm a princess.

We travel a while in silence, but for the occasional snort and pawing of the horses. White puffy clouds blow from their snouts as they make their way up the next incline.

"I probably should pull over and let them rest a minute."

Once we round the bend at the top of the crest, Mitch steers the team to the right toward a pull-off in the road, surrounded by a clump of pine trees.

He turns to me. "Are you too cold yet?"

I smile. "I could stand some hot chocolate or a mocha, but I'm all right."

"Well, we can do that, you know, once we get back. Head up to Cool Beanz."

I grin. "You've thought it all out, have you?"

"Do you mind?"

"No. This is nice, Mitch. Really nice."

He looks up at the starry skies. "You know, Gwen, I really want this business to make it."

"I'm sure it will," I encourage.

"It has to, you know." He turns to me in all seriousness. "Candace stuck her neck out for me on this. If it weren't for her, this business would still be a dream. The truth is I've squandered more of my parents' money than I care to admit, and I want to show them I've changed."

I don't know what to say. His confession surprises me. I would never have expected him to share such intimate details of his life with me.

"After this morning in the service…well, I watched you during worship, and I knew then that you would understand." He studies me a moment. "I'm still trying to figure out where you fit into all of this, though."

"Me?" I give a nervous laugh.

"Yeah, I can't help feeling there's a reason you're here. Beyond spreading your wings."

"And what might that reason be?"

He shrugs. "I don't know. Maybe you're here to teach me something."

My spirit dips a little. I was hoping he'd think beyond that. But maybe he's right. Maybe I am here to help him in some way or vice versa. Time will tell, I guess. A gust of wind sails past us, causing me to shiver.

"Oh here, let me help you," Mitch says, scooting toward me. He pulls the blanket up farther around my shoulders, tucking it under my neck.

"Thanks," I say, looking at him.

He stays perfectly still, his eyes gazing into the deepest part of me. His right hand reaches up to my chin and lifts it a notch while his head inches toward me. My heart pauses while his lips touch mine. He pulls me lightly to him. I feel fragile and delicate. His hands work through my hair, causing my emotions to explode with the moment. When I finally break away we are both breathless.

His hands cup my face. "Whatever the reason, I'm glad you're here," he whispers.

As the minutes tick by, I'm not sure how I get home or into my room but when I snuggle beneath my blankets, there's one thing I do know. I will never forget this night.

Guacamole is sleeping when I slip out my door the next morning. Hopefully, he won't get into any trouble today, but if he does, at least we have no guests at present. That's hardly good news for Mitch, though.

"Good morning, Granny," I say as I walk toward the table.

"It's about time you came down for breakfast." Granny places the plate of pancakes in the center of the table.

I ignore her crusty comment. That's just Granny's way. "As delicious as that looks, I'm going to pass on it this morning. I think I'll simply drink a cup of coffee."

Granny's eyes narrow. "You sick?"

I smile and shake my head. I couldn't eat a bite if my life depended on it.

"When a girl can't eat, she's sick, plain and simple."

I shrug. "I'm not hungry. I don't know why."

The front door pushes open, and a gust of wind slips in with Mitch.

"Morning, all." He stomps the snow from his boots, then looks up at me. "Morning, Gwen."

Excitement surges through me, races to my feet, and causes my toes to curl again. If I keep this up, I'll have to order special shoes.

I smile.

Granny grunts. "No appetite, huh?" She makes that comment for my ears only then swishes past me toward the kitchen.

Mitch comes my way, and I'm hoping we'll share a comment or two about last night, confirming that it wasn't a dream.

"It's still snowing out there." Mitch's forehead is scrunched with worry.

Maybe it was a dream.

Granny steps back into the room with the syrup

and a plate of bacon, then sits down. Mitch and I do the same.

Granny takes one look at his face and says, "What's the matter?"

"I want it to stop snowing. People can't make it out to ski if it keeps up." His voice has a definite growl to it. Must not have slept much last night. I'm liking that idea, hoping I might have had something to do with that.

"Yes, but think of the business you'll have once it slows down a little and the mountain is covered with fresh snow." I take a deep breath and exhale. It's going to be a great day, I can feel it.

Mitch stares at me. "Fresh snow isn't exactly the best type to ski on." I'm detecting a bit of hostility here. Did somebody got up on the wrong side of bed this morning?

"Well, people could visit the shop, or take a romp through the woods as long as the weather isn't frigid."

He practically gapes at me. Granny, too.

"What?" I get the distinct impression that I've said something wrong here.

"Are you always this way?"

"What way?"

"Never mind. Granny, will you pray, please?"

Granny prays, but I don't hear it. I can't get past whatever it is I have done wrong. Once the prayer is over, Granny passes the pancakes and syrup. The sweet aroma hovers over the table. Silverware clinks against plates, and I sit in silence.

"Sure you don't want any?" Granny asks.

"No, thanks." Now I'm too perplexed to eat.

Mitch cuts a bite of pancake, soaks it in syrup and eats it. "You know the problem with you, Gwen, is you're too positive. You don't see things as they really are."

"Excuse me? I see things as they are—I merely refuse to dwell on the negative. Life holds so much potential." I smile, refusing to allow his downer attitude to suck me in.

"Is that what you think I do, dwell on the negative?"

"Well, you do tend to, um, worry about things." I take a sip of my drink, wishing I could be somewhere else right now because this conversation can't go any direction but south.

"I don't worry, Gwen. I'm a businessman and a realist. I see things as they are, and I deal with them. I can't walk around with my head in the clouds."

Granny isn't saying a word, but her face tells me she's enjoying this conversation.

"I don't walk around with my head in the clouds, Mitch." I struggle to keep my words at an even pitch.

He chuckles.

"Is something funny?" I'm definitely feeling offended here.

"Gwen, you'd look for the bright side of an avalanche."

"Is that so wrong?"

"I didn't say it was wrong, just not realistic."

"Oh, negative attitudes are so much better?"

"At least I can deal with the problems as they come, because I see them coming. You haven't a clue."

"You're right. I don't always see the negative things coming. As in this conversation. I hadn't expected it this morning. Now if you'll excuse me, I have work to do." I scoot from my chair and stomp off. I'm not sure whether to go to my room or out the door, but since I've made such a dramatic exit, I decide to snatch my coat from the closet and leave.

And that's exactly what I do. With all the flair of Scarlett O'Hara, I shrug on my coat, stomp through the door and yank it closed with a nice, dramatic slam. "There, that should teach them," I say with a snap of my head. I brush my gloved hands together and turn away from the door.

It's too early to go to work, but I guess I have no choice at this point. I can hardly go back inside. I make my way up to the ski lift. Maybe Mitch is in a bad mood because of what happened last night. He probably regrets it and doesn't want me to have any romantic notions about the two of us. One thing for sure, I certainly had envisioned a very different time at the breakfast table today.

Maybe I do walk around with my head in the clouds.

"I might as well go home," Lisa says, taking a final swipe at the polished butcher-block counter. "This place is dead."

"You know, I can't help feeling it's more than the snow." I tuck the notebook with the inventory and menu list under my arm and lean against one side of the counter.

She stops and turns to me. "What do you mean?"

"I can't put my finger on it." I think a moment. "I don't know much about skiing, but I wouldn't think there's so much snow that it would keep avid skiers from coming. Maybe I'll go down to Dream Slopes and see how they're doing."

"Oh, I'm sure they're struggling, too," Lisa jumps in.

"Maybe, but it wouldn't hurt to check it out. You want to come with me?"

"I—I've got some studying to do. I'd like to go home."

I shrug. "Suit yourself."

"You'd better be careful doing the private investigator thing. Snooping can get you into trouble."

I laugh. "I'm hardly Angela Lansbury. Just curious, that's all."

"Remember what that does to the cat?"

"Now you're starting to act like Mitch."

"How so?"

I think maybe I've said too much. I don't want to talk about Mitch to Lisa—or anyone for that matter. He's not only my boss, but—well, I don't know what else, but I do feel a certain loyalty to him.

"Oh, I don't know." I wave my arm and look around. "I suppose Mitch won't care if we close shop early. It's two o'clock. I'll go down and ask him. You go on home, Lisa. I can handle things here."

"Well, if you're sure."

I nod.

"I'll see you tomorrow."

I watch as Lisa pulls on her coat and hat and slips through the door with a final wave. Satisfied that the shop is clean, I pull on my coat and shove through the door. The snow seems to have slowed a little, but there's still hardly anyone on site today. It's very strange.

I head to the B and B and once I'm there, step inside. "Is Mitch around?" I call out to Granny, who's sitting on the sofa in the great room.

"He's around somewhere, but goodness knows where."

I take a deep breath. "There hasn't been any business in the shop for the last two hours—except for one man grabbing a quick sandwich. I'm going on an errand, and I'll be right back."

Granny nods, her knitting needles clacking away as she works with skillful hands on the baby blanket.

I turn around and close the door behind me. In no time, I'm pulling my car into the Dream Slopes parking lot. I'm stunned at what I see there. The place is packed. As I suspected, all this snow wouldn't keep away serious skiers. What's going on?

Once I get out of my car, I hear some young women a few feet away talking. The wind howls between us, making it hard to hear. I pull my scarf closer to my neck and try to edge up behind them. Maybe something they say will give me a clue as to why everyone is coming to Dream Slopes today instead of Windsor Mountain.

I lag behind, though all they're talking about at this point are boys and schoolwork. We edge closer to the ticket booth, and I don't have the money or the time to go inside, so I start to turn.

The ticket man says, "Do you have your coupon for the two-for-one deal?"

I swivel back around. The girl in front of me promptly displays a coupon of some type.

"Great." He rings up their ticket, and I stand gaping as they walk away, tickets in hand.

So that's it. A two-for-one deal. Monica is running a special. No wonder people are coming here today. Armed with information, I turn to go and plow into the person right behind me.

"Oh, I'm sorry," I say before I look into the face of the person I've plowed into.

"Hello, Gwen."

When I hear Mitch's voice and see his face, I seriously struggle to see the silver lining in this situation.

Something tells me I'm turning into a realist.

Chapter Twelve

"What are you doing here?" Mitch's frown puts me a little on the defensive.

"I can explain."

"That would be good." He nudges my arm and eases me away from other people, over to the side. "Is Lisa running the coffee shop?"

That whole optimist thing is just not happening for me here. I'm struggling to breathe, and my blood is moving past the simmering stage. I search for the words.

"Well, who's running the coffee shop, Gwen?" His voice moves up a pitch.

I stare at him. "I closed it."

With great labor, he exhales. "Oh, that's perfect. We have a little downtime, and you think you can close the shop." He stares back at me.

I start to talk but all I do is let out a squeak. I'm

speechless, totally speechless. Trust me, this doesn't happen often. But when I find my voice, Mitch had better look out.

He crosses his arms over his chest, his eyebrows plunge and his lips are scrunched.

I refuse to let him intimidate me. I lift my chin. "I thought I would—"

"Oh, Mitch, there you are." Monica waltzes up to us like a breeze. I want to huff and puff and blow her into the next county. I know that's not the best of attitudes, but it's all I'm coming up with at the moment.

Her presence catches him off guard. He drops his arms. Suddenly his voice is filled with concern. "Hi, Monica. I got over here as fast as I could."

She looks at me and smiles sweetly. For some reason, I can't get past the feeling that she's tattled on me.

"If you'll excuse us, Gwen?" She's already tugging on Mitch's arm and pulling him away from me. She obviously doesn't realize she's doing me a favor.

I turn to go. "We'll talk later," Mitch says, letting me know this matter isn't over yet.

I'm mad enough to spit.

I clean the last dribble of milk from the counter, and the coffee shop sparkles. I haven't seen Mitch at all today. He hasn't talked to me over what happened at Dream Slopes yesterday. It's just as well. I was too angry to talk about it then. And I never get angry—well, hardly ever.

Putting away the mocha mix, I check through the bottles of flavoring to make sure they're all in order. I think I spent the entire afternoon yesterday counting coffee beans. I had everything else done and only three customers came in for coffee. That's it. But of course Mitch still wanted me there. Who would have believed I'd go from a respectable fifth grade teacher to counting coffee beans? I've got to wonder what I'm doing here. Is this truly stretching my wings, or am I wasting time?

A handful of customers push through the coffee shop, stomping snow from their boots, shaking their hats and scarves, stopping a moment by the fireplace to rub their hands together and get warm. Lisa and I prepare their drinks, and they talk quietly at their tables, finish their drinks, then leave. The room is silent once again.

"You know, I have some studying to do. Since things are slow again, would you mind if I go in the back room a while? If we get customers, yell, and I'll come back out to help."

"Okay, I'll handle things and call you if I need you."

"Thanks." Lisa disappears into the back room.

If there's one thing I can't stand, it's boredom. I've had enough of that in the last two days to last me a while. I've already taken inventory, ordered supplies, checked over the menu, and there's nothing left to do. We've got to think of something to stir up business.

I make myself a mocha, grab my cup, some paper and a pen, then head for the table to do some serious thinking. Before I can sit down, the door opens and Mitch walks inside.

"Can we talk?"

That's a good sign. He didn't say "we need to talk" but rather "can we talk." I'm seeing this as a positive thing.

"Sure. You want something to drink?"

"No. I don't have time."

So much for being positive. Stress has now entered his face, and I feel a lecture coming on.

"First off, I want to know why you were at Dream Slopes yesterday when you were supposed to be running the coffee shop."

I swallow hard. Then I swallow again for good measure. "I went there because I wanted to see how their business was doing. When I saw all the cars there, I decided to check it out. Sure enough, they were running a special."

"Yeah, the special we had talked about running

next week." He looks at me. "The special *you* had suggested, as a matter of fact."

"Right." I can't help wondering what he's implying here.

"How odd that she would do that right at this time." He stares at me.

"Isn't it, though?" I stare back.

He clears his throat, looks away a moment, then turns back to me. "I've had some complaints this morning—about the coffee."

Oh, goody, we're going from bad to worse. "And?"

"They said they could get a better cup of coffee at the local gas station."

If he doesn't stop filling my head with all this good news, there will be just no living with me.

"Did you hear me?"

"Yes, I heard you." I pause. "If they didn't like their coffee, why didn't they come back up and tell us? We would have made it right."

He leans toward me here. "The point is, Gwen, it should have been right the first time."

"Look, Mitch, we're doing the best we can. If we made a mistake, we're sorry."

"*We* didn't make a mistake. *You* did."

My tongue sticks to the roof of my mouth.

"They described the woman who made it for them. It was you."

"I'd offer you my firstborn, but I have no children."

"This isn't a joke, Gwen."

"Well, what do you want from me, Mitch? I didn't mean to make a bad cup of coffee, but if I did, there's not much I can do about it to make it right if they don't come back up and tell me."

He takes off his gloves and runs his fingers through his hair. "I don't know, Gwen." He sounds defeated and my heart aches for him a little. But not too much. After all, he hasn't exactly been on my side lately. "I don't mean to take it out on you. I know your coffee is normally great. Maybe you were distracted or something? I just can't afford to have disgruntled patrons. If this business doesn't get off the ground…" His words fall with his expression.

"What? You're ready to give up with the first sign of struggle? What's up with that? I mean, either you're committed to this business or you're not." I'm surprising myself here with my boldness, but hey, I'm on a roll. Mitch looks as though he's been splashed in the face with cold water. I trudge forward. "It's time to be creative, Mitch. Offer something else rather than slicing fees, if you're worried about the money. How about an educational tour of some type for students? Teach children about survival in the snow, talk about how people in the nineteenth century struggled in the wilderness areas. Lure in the honeymooners with candlelight dinners, romantic music, sleigh rides."

He holds up his hand when I take a breath. I'm totally silent while he sits there with his hand in the air resembling an Indian statue.

"Where does all that come from?"

"Huh?"

"I mean, where do you get all these ideas?"

I perk. "It's in my nature." I'm smiling here. He's not.

Okay, tense moment. "I think we can do more," I say, meaning *we* as in our team, and I'm hoping he takes it that way.

"Yeah, I guess you're right."

Now, we're making a little headway. He's starting to calm down and actually listen. The coffee shop door opens, and an employee enters.

"Hi, Mitch. Granny told me to tell you that the guy who runs the rope tow had to leave."

He blows out a sigh. "Great. That's just great." His gaze meets mine, then he turns back to the employee. "Thanks," he says, pretty much dismissing the guy.

He turns to me again. "See, that's what I mean. How can I run a business without reliable employees? First you leaving your post yesterday, and now he's going home. See what you did, Gwen? You set a bad example."

My mouth gapes. "How can you pin this on me? This is ridiculous. I told you why I left here yesterday."

"Yes, you told me a *version* of your story."

"And what does *that* mean?"

"It means I'm not fully convinced that's the truth, that's what that means." His face is red, and he's rising from the chair. I get up, too.

"Well, whether you believe me or not doesn't change the fact that it is the truth, Mitch Windsor."

"Well, truth or not, see that it doesn't happen again. In the future if you need to leave your post, you had better check with me before doing so." With that he spins around and stomps out the door.

My voice catches in my throat again. I can hardly believe what's happened here.

"Are you all right?"

I turn around to see Lisa standing at the counter.

"I don't get him at all." The floorboards creak beneath me as I pace across the room. "I'm trying to help him, and he's practically ready to fire me because of it!" My voice rises in pitch. I'm working myself up good. Mitch Windsor seems to bring that out in me. I've said it before, but it bears repeating: it takes a lot to get me stirred up, but I could rival an Arizona dust storm right about now.

"He's stressed. I wouldn't let it worry you."

"Well, that's easy for you to say—you're not the one he's mad at."

She looks at me.

"I'm sorry. I didn't mean to snap at you. I'm a little upset."

"It's all right. I understand. It's hard to be happy when people betray you and hurt you."

"Who said anything about betraying? Did I say he betrayed me?"

"Well, no, but I meant in general."

I'm not exactly in the mood for Dr. Phil. "He hasn't betrayed me, but I'm certainly feeling the brunt of his frustrations right now."

I start to tell her about the coffee complaints, but several patrons enter the shop, and we get back to making drinks. I take extra care in preparation since I've had complaints. I can't imagine what I did wrong before with the coffee, unless I had my mind on Mitch instead of what I was doing. I guess that's possible.

Never mind the earlier complaints. I think I'd rather go back to counting beans.

By the time I've finished work and head for the B and B, I'm fairly drained. The exhaustion comes more from the emotional stress, I'm sure, than the actual physical work at Cool Beanz today.

I come from a well-adjusted family. Okay, aside from that whole grandchild obsession my parents have going on. I've never heard my parents raise their voices. I have more of a temper than my parents, and I have practically nil.

I'm feeling a bit persecuted. I mean, here I was trying to help Mitch and things turned south. I don't get it.

Once inside the house, I take off my coat, hat and gloves and slip them into the closet. I climb the stairs and step into my room. When I'm about to close the door, I hear Granny and Mitch talking down the hall. I shamelessly leave the door open a crack.

"I don't know what to think, Granny. Between that nosy reptile getting loose, Gwen making bad coffee and then showing up at Dream Slopes—well, I don't know."

"Mitch, you know she isn't doing any of that on purpose."

Mitch runs his hand through his hair. "I know it doesn't make sense. I should talk to Candace about it."

"She would have nothing to gain," Granny adds. They step around and edge down the stairs, their voices fading with them.

"Unless—" Mitch's words are lost on me. I can't hear him no matter how hard I strain. Unless what? What was he going to say? Does he honestly think I would hurt his business on purpose? I close the door, walk over to my bed and fall onto it.

Lord, I don't know what to do here. I've made such a mess of things, and I didn't mean to. You know that. You're the only One who knows the truth and knows what's going on. Please help me to do the right thing to help Mitch. Amen.

After my prayer, I fall asleep. The next thing I know, someone is knocking at my door. I rub my eyes and look at my watch. It's eight o'clock. Taking a quick peek at myself in the mirror, I straighten my hair then walk to the door.

"Oh, uh, I didn't know if you were in there or not. You didn't come down for dinner, and I—" Mitch clears his throat here. "I mean, Granny and I, we were sort of worried about you."

"You're worried about *me?*" I stare at him until he squirms. He gets my drift. I start to close the door. He stops it with his hand.

"Look, Gwen, I'm sorry. I've been a little edgy lately, and—"

"A little?"

"All right, a lot. I've been upset about the business, and I've taken it out on you. Will you forgive me?" He lifts my chin with his hand, sending chills through me yet again.

My eyes meet his.

"Please?"

I crack a smile, a tiny one, mind you. "Yes."

Obvious relief shines through his eyes. "Are you hungry?"

I'm still a little hesitant.

"Gwen?" His eyes implore me to forgive him.

"Well, now that you mention it, I guess I am a little hungry."

He grins. "Believe it or not, I actually saved you some of Granny's chicken potpie. It's my favorite, so count yourself lucky." He stretches out his hand for mine. My heart thumps against my chest. I swallow hard. He takes my hand into his and leads me downstairs. A hundred electrical impulses spark through my arm. When we get downstairs, Granny leaves the kitchen and enters the dining room. Mitch drops my hand. "I'll be right back. I'll get your meal for you."

I'm positively speechless. He's fetching dinner for me? He is *so* back on the pedestal.

Granny sits across from me while Mitch is in the kitchen. She makes quick small talk then gets to the point. "How good are you at mending clothes?"

"Excuse me?"

"Mending. You ever do any mending? You know, replace a button, sew a ripped seam, let out a hem, that type of thing?"

"I do some. I'm not a seamstress, if that's what you mean, but I manage to take care of my own mending. If it's too detailed, though, I take my garments to a professional for alterations."

Granny nods her approval. Mitch enters the room and she leaves. I can't help wondering what that was all about. But I don't dwell on it, since I've entered the Cinderella portion of my evening. Mitch sits across from me at the table after he's served me my meal and offered a prayer for the food.

"You know, I was thinking I'd like to start meeting with you and Granny on Monday and Friday mornings for business meetings," he says.

I want to savor the creamy gravy that's in the potpie, but I can't show him my excitement over food. I nod.

"You came up with some pretty good ideas earlier, and I'd like to discuss them in more detail at the meetings and maybe come up with some more."

The reality of this moment hits me. Wait. I don't do reality, do I? Mitch says no. Still, here it is in black and white. Reality. My spirits plunge. He served my meal so he could talk me into a business meeting. Well, now, that does wonders for the ego. "What time and where do you want to meet?" I manage after I take a drink of iced tea.

"Let's plan on Monday and Friday mornings at seven-thirty, and we'll meet in the conference room."

"I'll be there."

"That will give us all the weekend to come up with some more ideas and discuss the ones you mentioned. We'll then work on implementing each one, setting a scheduled date, that kind of thing."

I keep eating, listening to his plans. When he's finished talking, I look up. "Sounds good."

"Great." His old enthusiasm is back in place. "Well, I'll let you eat in peace." He gets up from the table and exits the room, leaving me alone with my meal and my thoughts.

And they say women are moody....

Chapter Thirteen

I stop typing on the computer long enough to take a drink of hot tea and rub the back of my neck. I'm tired, but at least the scent of the cinnamon candle flickering on the table makes me feel better.

A week has passed, and we've had one business meeting since Mitch and I talked. Granny said the day the high schoolers came to the resort went well. They did quite a bit of business at Cool Beanz, and there were plenty of kids skiing. She liked my idea of teaching children about survival in the snow and nineteenth-century folks living in the wilderness areas.

Mitch suggested we take that idea and run with it. I've been talking with school corporations in the vicinity to see if we might offer our services in this way. They seem to like the idea. Now

Mitch has Lisa and a neighbor covering Cool Beanz in the afternoons while I put together a curriculum of some type for elementary kids to use in conjunction with our ski resort.

"You need to take a break," Granny says, bringing a fresh mug of tea.

"Thanks, Granny."

"You're a hard worker, you know."

"I've been accused of that before," I say with a smile.

Granny stares at me a moment, hands on her hips. "How do you remove stains?"

What in the world? Where did that come from? "Excuse me?"

"On your clothes, how do you get out stains?"

Are we on *Candid Camera* here? I look around and see nothing out of the ordinary. "Uh, I usually soak garments in a stain-removal liquid."

"Does it work?"

"Most of the time," I say, wondering what this is all about.

"That's how you save money, you know. You can't go out and buy new clothes every time you get a stain on something." She adds a grunt at the end of her comment and leaves the room.

Now, I like Granny, I really do, but she does strike me as being a little, well, eccentric.

Mitch steps through the front door. "How's it

going?" The glow on his face is back in place, and he's smiling. Now all is right with my world.

"It's going fine. I think in a couple of days I'll have something to show the school corps."

"That's my girl," he says, then his face turns fiery red. "I mean, um, I meant to say—"

"Well, what's the matter, boy, spit it out," Granny says, entering the room. I don't think she has a clue what he's said to me.

"Granny, what's for dinner?" He totally changes the subject, and I have to swallow my giggle.

Granny blinks and scratches her head. "Well, we're having steak, mashed potatoes and gravy, green beans, salad, dinner rolls. Is that all right with you?" Her eyes sparkle with mischief.

Mitch relaxes. "Sounds great."

"How's everything going at Cool Beanz?" I ask while Mitch takes off his coat and finds a seat at my table.

"Going well." A twinge of disappointment niggles at me. Not that I want to work at Cool Beanz forever, but, well, it's a little humbling to know I'm so easily replaced.

"Great." I don't want to show what a slug I truly am.

"So you and Lisa are getting to be pretty good friends, huh?" Mitch stretches back, tipping his chair on its hind legs. He rests his hands behind his head and smiles.

"Yeah, I guess we are. We're going out for coffee after dinner tonight."

"You don't get enough of that during the day?" He laughs.

"Well, sometimes it's nice to go out and let someone serve us for a change." I grin.

"I'm sure you're good for her."

"How do you mean?"

"Oh, I don't know. I get the feeling she's got some issues."

"Really?" I think it's kind of amusing that he's saying that, because guys rarely notice anything beyond the surface—well, it seems that way most of the time.

He shrugs. "Call it a hunch."

Is he warning me to be careful? I want to ask him if he's being my protector, but he might say no, and then I'd feel stupid. "It's nice to have someone to hang out with. Lauren's often busy with her own family, and I don't want to bother her all the time."

He nods, drops his chair to the floor, his arms to his side, and leans into the table. "So you say you think you'll have something for the schools in a couple of days?"

"Uh-huh."

"That's great. The sooner, the better." He pauses a moment. "Well, I guess I'd better get back out there." He stands up, puts his coat back on and walks through the door.

As I watch him leave, I whisper a prayer for Mitch and his resort. I know it's important for him to make this work.

"I wonder if it will ever stop snowing," I say when Lisa and I enter the downtown coffee shop. It's a cozy little place. The baristas work in a fairly confined space, and beyond the counter there are only about six tables and a couple of overstuffed brown chairs by a warm fireplace. It's a cute place, not to mention the fact that I don't have to work here.

We both stomp the snow from our boots at the door then walk over to the counter.

"Still not used to this weather, huh?" Lisa teases.

"I haven't thawed out since I moved here."

Lisa laughs. We place our orders, get our drinks and walk over to a table.

"I guess since I've lived here all my life, the snow doesn't bother me all that much."

"Yeah, you'd probably have a problem with the cactus and scorpions out our way," I say with a laugh.

She wrinkles her nose. "Don't want to go there."

We pause a moment. "So how are the business sessions going with Mitch?" Lisa asks.

"Well, we've only had one, but it was fine, I guess. We're trying to come up with something for the school systems in the area." I proceed to tell her about our plan to implement a class for elementary kids.

"Wow, that's a great idea, Gwen! I can tell you're a teacher. That should help business."

"We sure hope so."

"When do you think you'll be finished so you can take it to the schools?"

"I should be done in a couple of days and hope to schedule appointments right after that. We'd like to have something lined up in the next week or two."

"Super." Lisa takes a drink from her cup then wipes her mouth with a napkin. "Hey, I've been meaning to ask you how the vertigo thing is now."

I stir the whipped cream into my mocha and replace the lid. "It's great as long as I don't look down. If I look down, I'm sunk." I take another drink.

"You know, there's a clinic around here that deals with that kind of thing."

"Oh?"

"Yeah, it's a three-day deal where they say they can get you past that."

"In three days?"

"I know it sounds strange, but a girl I go to school with has been there, and she says it really works. You ought to check it out."

I shrug. "I don't know."

"Well, it couldn't hurt. I mean, didn't you say that the doctors couldn't find anything physically wrong with you?"

"Yeah."

"So it must be something emotional."

"Well, I guess it could be, but I can't imagine what. I mean, wouldn't I know that?"

"Not always. It could be a childhood trauma that you've suppressed or something weird like that."

"Thanks."

We both laugh. "I didn't mean that you were weird, I only meant—oh, I don't know, the human mind and all that is so hard to figure out."

"Yeah, that's true."

"Sometimes, I don't know why I do the things I do."

"You, too? I think it's a woman thing," I say with a laugh.

"Maybe. Still, I wish—" She stops short and studies her fingers. I wait. She finally looks up at me. "I don't always know how to be a good friend, you know?" Her gaze is fixed on mine.

"I understand. I have my struggles with that, too. We're human, and we make mistakes. Besides, I think you're a great friend."

"Thanks." She lowers her head and nods. Something tells me that Mitch is right. She has some issues in her past, and maybe it involves a friend. I don't want to pry, so I decide to pray for her. I'll talk to her when the time is right.

The next couple of days pass without incident, which means I've managed not to break anything, and Guacamole actually stays in my room. This morning we have guests at the inn, and they join us for breakfast.

"So nice to have you with us," Mitch says to the man sitting across from him.

"We're enjoying ourselves immensely," he responds while spreading jelly across his biscuit.

"I must say we're looking forward to skiing on your mountain," his wife cuts in. "We were at Dream Slopes yesterday."

I glance at Mitch and see his body stiffen ever so slightly at the mention of Dream Slopes.

"It's very nice, too. We met the owner, Monica something-or-other." The woman waves her hand for emphasis. "I think it's really wonderful that she's offering a class for the schools. It's always good to reach out to the community."

Granny drops her fork, causing it to make a loud clang against her plate.

The woman jumps. "Oh, dear."

My gaze collides with Mitch. The weird thing about it is I get the feeling I've done something wrong. Why is that?

He turns back to the woman. "That is a good idea."

She smiles as though she's on to something. "You should try it. It might help you out here, too."

"As a matter of fact, we're already working on something similar."

"Oh, dear. I guess the competition beat you to the punch," she says with a hearty laugh, not realizing how upsetting her comment is to the rest of us—well, excluding her husband.

"If you all will excuse me," Mitch says, "I'd better get to work." He turns to me. "Gwen, could I talk to you a minute, please?"

Uh-oh, here we go again. I've never been called to the principal's office, but I suspect it feels just about this way.

"I want you to give it to me straight. Did you talk to Monica Howell about this?"

My jaw drops. I mean, literally, it falls as far as it can without popping out of socket.

"Gwen, I asked you a question."

"You're kidding, right?"

"Do I look like I'm kidding?"

He has me there. "Why would I do that, Mitch?"

He folds his arm across his chest and taps his toe. I'm beginning to recognize and dislike this stance.

"You haven't answered my question."

"I shouldn't have to. You should trust me more than that. But since you need an answer, I'll give you one. No, I have not talked with Monica Howell. We're not exactly close friends. That would be *your* department." I turn on my heels and stomp away—well, walk away hard enough to get my point across without alarming our guests.

I then hear Mitch leave the house.

By the time I get up to my room, my hands are shaking. I've never been accused of anything like that before. What makes it worse is the pain. It hurts that Mitch doesn't trust me. It hurts because I realize something I've been trying to ignore since the day I arrived here.

I care about Mitch Windsor, much more than I want to, and he sees me merely as a threat to his business.

The day doesn't get any better. I've made one mistake after another, it's freezing cold outside, and I want to go home. I consider calling Lauren, but I don't want to bother her merely so she can hear me whine.

After dinner, I offer to help Granny clean up the dishes. She's a little more open to help now. I think it's only because her arthritis is acting up again.

"Thank you for helping me, kiddo," Granny says, finishing up the last few plates.

"I'm glad to help." The truth be known, Granny's presence comforts me somehow. Maybe it's because she's older or reminds me of home in some way. I don't know.

"Don't be so hard on yourself. The truth will come out in the end."

I reach for a wet plate and her comment shakes me a moment. The plate slips between my fingers and crashes onto the floor. Right now I want to crawl in a hole and stay there.

"What—"

I turn to see Mitch standing in the doorway. Great. Just great.

He sighs and turns back around.

I get on my hands and knees to pick up the fragmented china, thankful for the chance to hide my eyes, which are welling up with tears.

"These dishes are too old anyway. I've told Mitch a hundred times he needs to get something new, more cheerful. You know, some of that red cherry stuff that you like."

Tears plop onto the floor, and I quickly wipe them with my towel.

Granny lowers onto the floor. I know this is a gesture of friendship, because her arthritis makes such an act painful. Her gnarled hand grabs mine. "Don't you worry. It's only a plate. Broken plates can be replaced. Broken hearts, not so easily."

I'm not sure what she means, but I suspect she knows how I feel about Mitch, and she feels sorry for me. I appreciate her concern, but I don't want her pity.

Her kind, faded blue eyes look into mine. "He'll come around, you'll see."

I nod and go back to picking up the plate pieces, wondering exactly what her comment means. "He'll come around," as in he'll understand that I wouldn't betray him like that, or "he'll come around," as in he'll see how much I care about him and grow to care about me, too? I sigh. I'm tired of trying to analyze everything.

Once the mess is cleaned up, I go to my room and the phone rings. "Hello?"

"How's my baby girl?"

I wipe my nose and try to hide any indication that I've been crying. "Dad! So good to hear from you. How are you and Mom?" I'm careful here. I don't want them to know that I'm homesick. They should be free to live their own lives and not have to worry about their adult daughter.

"We're getting along fine," Dad says.

"We've having such fun seeing all the sights, Gwen," Mom joins in.

They tell me about their travels out West and everything they've been doing for the past couple of weeks. A knot the size of Texas forms in my throat, but I refuse to surrender to it. I want them to be happy, and I have to learn to stand on my own two feet.

I tell them how things are going—well, I leave out the grisly details, and they seem satisfied. We end the conversation pleasantly enough, and I think I've convinced them that everything is going well.

I grab my journal and decide I'd like to stretch out on the window seat downstairs. It's a perfect place for writing. It offers a scenic view, and my sweater will shield me from any drafts.

After getting a cup of hot chocolate with marsh-mallows, I scoot onto the window seat with my journal. I tuck my pen and journal in the corner of the nook, and I cradle the mug of hot choco-late in my hands. Though I hate the cold, I have to admit the scene outside the window thrills me. It's picture perfect. Where you couldn't manufac-ture or work up the feeling the scene brings to you, no matter how hard you tried? That's the one. I sit there a moment soaking it up.

Finally, I push my mug aside. I pick up my journal and pen and begin to write….

Chapter Fourteen

It's easy to be inspired when I see scenes like this, Father. It makes me wonder why I take so long to write my thoughts to You. I can think much more clearly on paper.

Many things on my mind these days. Vertigo continues to plague me. I wonder if there's any truth to what Lisa said about it possibly being a problem from my past. Should I check out the clinic, Lord? I'm open to that if it will help me. I wouldn't care so much if I weren't in this business, but if I'm going to stay here—and that looks a bit debatable at the moment—then I need to get over this vertigo/fear of heights thing.

I don't know what's going on with Monica, how she's beating us to the punch on business things, but You know. Mitch seems to take his frustrations out on me. I suspect that Monica is playing that Samson and Delilah game. If Mitch is dumb enough to surrender to it, then he deserves everything he's getting. Maybe I shouldn't be saying this in prayer, but You know my heart anyway, Lord. I'm sorry for the jealousy. Help me know what to do here and to do my best.

"Can I interrupt you a moment?" Mitch startles me, and I turn to see him standing there, gazing at me. His fingers fiddle with the gloves he's holding.

"Yeah." I close my journal, and he steps closer.

"There's no excuse for the way I've been acting toward you lately. I wouldn't blame you if you never spoke to me again, but I just had to say— once again—that I'm sorry. I shouldn't allow the pressure of running this place get to me."

I'm not sure what to say, so I keep silent.

"I'm frustrated by everything. It's obvious one of my employees is trying to ruin me. Maybe I'm not cut out for this business."

"I don't think that's true, Mitch. I think you are a fine businessman."

He looks at me as though I've handed him a lifeline. "Thanks, Gwen."

Self-consciousness invades me, and my gaze lowers to the closed journal in my lap.

"Well, I guess I'll let you get back to your writing. I only wanted to tell you I'm sorry. I'll try to do better." He turns to go.

"Mitch?"

He swivels back around.

"Thanks."

He lifts a smile then leaves the room, taking my heart with him.

Somehow we survived the rest of last week, despite Monica's constant interruptions, showing up unannounced. Mitch continues to meet with her now and then, and none of that makes sense to me.

By the time we're halfway through this week, snow returns with a vengeance. Mitch refuses to take the hit this time. Without announcing it in our business meeting, he runs a two-for-one special. I'm happy that his decision brings in more customers, but I can't help feeling slighted that he didn't reveal his plans to me. There's definitely a trust issue here, but I don't know what to do about it.

Lisa and I have more customers than we can keep up with today, thanks to the special. I'm not complaining, though—at least we're keeping busy.

By day's end, I'm tired and ready to go back to the B and B. After dinner, I decide to go to bed early and start reading a good book.

"Hey, I'm going to watch a Jerry Lewis/Dean Martin movie, want to join me?" Mitch looks gorgeous in his khaki pants and navy sweater against a backdrop of pine bookshelves and a winter snow scene beyond the windows. My heart has the wings of a butterfly.

I stare at him.

"You do know who they are, don't you?"

I smile. "Of course I do. I remember my parents watching their movies."

"Ouch."

I laugh. "I didn't mean it that way."

"So what do you say?"

I think a moment.

"Come on. I could use the company."

Is this a date? After all we've been going through lately, do I want this? Duh. No-brainer here. Yes, I want this. "All right."

"Great!" He rubs his hands together.

"I need to go to my room for a minute and check on Guacamole, then I'll be back."

His left eyebrow shoots up. "Oh, good idea." He grins. "I'll go make us some popcorn and get something to drink."

Glancing at the snow scene behind him, my insides now the consistency of baby food, I take one more glance at Hunky Boy and think my life could be on the verge of improving. I don't want to analyze it and ruin everything. For now I'll release my happy self and enjoy the evening with Mitch Windsor.

We watch the movie, laugh together, eat popcorn, and I think my life is definitely on the upswing. Granny walks into the room.

"Gwen, I need some help with the biscuits in the morning. Can't keep up with all these extra guests."

"Sure, I can do that, Granny. Lisa is scheduled to work early, so she can open Cool Beanz."

Granny looks relieved. I figure her arthritis is acting up again. Poor thing.

We go back to the movie, which ends all too quickly. Mitch clicks the button on the remote and turns off the TV. We sit in the silence a moment, listening only to the crackle of the nearby fireplace. I want to snuggle next to him, savor a cashew or two.

Mitch turns to face me. "We had a good day today. The special lured them in."

"Yeah, it was good."

"I have more reasons than money pushing me to make this business work, Gwen."

He's making himself vulnerable here, so I listen, knowing this is important.

"I've told you before I'm not proud of my past. I've let my parents down more times than I care to admit." He stares into the hearth's flames. "I don't blame them for not trusting me anymore, but I want to show them I've changed. For the first time in my life, I care more about doing a good job than I care about myself."

"That's cool, Mitch."

He shrugs. "Let's hope I can do it."

"Some things we can't do on our own. But we know the One who will help us."

"Yeah." He grabs my hand and looks at me. "I'm glad you're here." He gives my hand a squeeze, but before I can work up a full toe curl, he lets go.

We both get up and clean the dishes from the area. Once that's finished, he turns to me. "See you in the morning." I watch after him as he leaves the room.

There is a twinge of disappointment. Hello? Earth to Mitch Windsor. Ever heard of a good-night kiss? Of course you have. So where is it, Big Boy? Lay one on me, now! I shrug. I guess I can't have everything. As I climb the stairs to my room, I can't help wondering why Mitch didn't try to kiss me this time. Maybe there's something wrong with me. I stop on the stairway. Maybe he's changed his mind about me and thinks of me like a sister. Oh, that makes me feel better. Right.

I trudge on ahead. What's up with me? I'm don't usually have such negative thoughts. I think Mitch is rubbing off on me.

I get ready for bed, explain my frustrations to Guacamole and climb beneath my covers. Tonight I refuse to dwell on "what might be" reality. I choose to think positive. Life is exciting, every inch of it, and my heart thumps with the endless possibilities. I close my eyes and smile, hoping for the possibility that Mitch Windsor will invade my dreams.

The next morning I get up early and go downstairs to help Granny with the biscuits. Actually, I make the biscuits while Granny concentrates on the rest of the meal. Once we're finished with the preparations, we sit at the breakfast table together before the guests gather in the dining room.

"Wow, Gwen, did you make these?" Mitch points to the biscuit that now has teeth marks in it from his first bite.

Heat climbs my face and I nod.

"These are fantastic." He puts a glob of jelly on the remainder and plops it into his mouth with a grin.

I'm hoping Granny doesn't mind his compliment. I sneak a glance at her. I'm surprised when I see a smile on her face and a twinkle in her eye. Yet when she sees me looking, she turns all serious.

"So, what Scriptures are you reading?" Granny asks.

"Well, I'm reading about Esther right now. I love her story, how she was placed in a strategic position at an important time. Like that Wayne

Watson song, what's it called? 'For Such a Time as This'?"

"I don't know about that, but I enjoy the book of Esther, too," Granny says. "That girl had a good head on her shoulders."

I scoop some scrambled eggs with my fork. "We're not all called to do great things." I shrug. "I think it's equally important to be obedient in the small things. Speaking up when I need to, taking a stand, or being silent when I need to listen." I put the fork in my mouth and glance up. By Granny and Mitch's expressions, I'm thinking I must have sounded like I'm preaching or something, because they give me a sort of funny stare.

"Glad to see you're learning from her."

I'm not sure how to take that, but when Granny winks at me, I figure everything's fine, so I don't worry about it anymore.

After breakfast, I saunter up to Cool Beanz and join Lisa in the frenzy of activity. Another busy day. I love it.

Once we get a lull in the afternoon, we sit down and take a break.

"Hey, I wrote down the name of that clinic for you," Lisa says, shoving a piece of paper in my direction.

I see the clinic name on the paper, along with the phone number. "Thanks."

"I'm not trying to push you into going, Gwen. I'm only saying if you ever want to get to the bottom of the problem, they might be able to help you."

I sigh. "I know you're right. I'm not sure I want to deal with it right now." Noticing a coffee stain on my pant leg, I try to rub it off with my fingernail, but it refuses to leave. I cross my legs to hide it.

"I understand. Say, do you want to get together for dinner Friday night, maybe go shopping or something?"

"Sounds like fun." I'm really enjoying our times together. I make a mental note to call Lauren, too. It's been a while since we've gotten together. This is a busy time for their B and B.

"Uh-oh, that man left his keys in here," Lisa says, pointing to a glob of keys on a nearby table. "I told my professor I would call her promptly at three o'clock, so I have to make that call now. Can you get those to him?"

"Sure," I say, getting up to retrieve the keys and my coat.

"I'll watch the shop. If we get any customers, I'll tell my professor I'll call her back."

"Thanks," I call over my shoulder. A blustery gust of wind hits me and blows my hair all over my face. I wonder if I should go back into the shop and get my hat, but decide I won't be out here long enough to worry with it.

I look for the guy with the red hat. I remember he was the one with the keys, because he fidgeted with them while I was getting his drink. And since I'm crazy about red, I noticed his hat. I spot him, and my stomach coils. He's at the top of the mountain, getting ready to go down the slope. See, when I report for work, I don't have far to walk from the ski lift to get to Cool Beanz, so I can handle that. But to actually walk across the mountaintop where I can see the earth below… I have to wonder if I really want to do this.

I mean, he can come and get his own keys, right? Is it my fault he behaved irresponsibly? I'm thinking no. We're a coffee shop, not a pre-school. My thoughts wrestle about. I scan the mountaintop once more and take a deep breath.

The truth is it's not that far away, right, Lord? This is no big deal. I can do this. Feel free to stop me at any time.

Gathering my courage, I keep my focus forward, not daring to look to my right, which, of course, leads to the base of the mountain. "Keys, give him the keys," I mutter under my breath. I consider crawling on the ground. Hey, it works for Guacamole. But then I figure people might recognize me from the coffee shop and wonder what kind of help Mitch has hired.

My courage mounts with every step—well, a little bit, anyway. Keeping my focus forward…this will be a piece of cake. I love when I talk to myself this way, because cake always makes me feel better.

By the time I'm a few yards away from the man, he's in position to head down the slope. I yell at him, but of course I don't know his name, so it's one of those, "Hey, you with the red hat," calls, and he doesn't pay any attention to me.

Without thinking I watch him fly off in perfect form, when the swirling begins. Panic hits me, and I immediately plop to the ground so I won't fall. Swirling, swirling. I tip over then back again. Everything around me is topsy-turvy. I don't know how close I am to the edge. What if I tumble down the mountain? Panic clutches my throat and takes my breath away. The air is so thin. I try to pull myself into a fetal position, but I'm not sure if I'm doing it or not.

"Ma'am, are you all right?"

"Coffee shop. Lisa," I manage without throwing up. I hear people shuffling around me, eyeballs everywhere, looking down at me. *Oh, God, please help me.*

"Gwen, I'm here." It's not Lisa's voice but Mitch's. Great. He would have to see this.

"Don't lift me. Don't lift me," I shriek.

"I won't." His arms scoop around me and pull me toward him. He drags me across the ground. I squeeze my eyes tightly closed. My throat constricts as I try to breathe.

"Gwen, you're all right. Take a deep breath."

Without a tracheotomy, it's not happening.

"We're on the ground. You won't fall. I promise. I've got you, and I won't let you go." I might enjoy this at another point in time, but right now, well, it's just not doing it for me.

"Oh, my goodness, here, let me help." I hear Lisa. Her hands grip me, and the coffeehouse door creaks open as they lift me inside and slide me a few feet across the tiled floor. When I inhale, my breath rattles in my chest.

"I can take care of her from here," Mitch says once we're inside. He holds me tight. I'm thinking vertigo has its merits, though I'm not entirely convinced. Long, deep breaths. "It's going to be all right, Gwen." Whispered words calm me. My equilibrium settles into place. "We're in the coffee shop, nowhere near the heights."

Once my world is righted again I see that there are no customers in the shop, which makes me feel hugely better. We're still on the floor, Mitch and I. My back is to him and his arms are tight around my shoulders, my head in the curve of his neck. I'm thinking I could stay here a while and pretend to still be fighting vertigo, but there's that whole honesty issue.

I reluctantly squirm and admit to feeling better. Mitch releases his hold, doggone it.

I don't miss the smirk on Lisa's face. She knows I was enjoying that little moment.

Mitch smoothes my hair. He turns me around to look into my eyes. "Are you better now?"

I swallow. Hard. "Yes. Thanks, Mitch."

His gaze doesn't leave me. It's intent, burning a hole through my heart. "I hate to see you suffer like that, Gwen. You need to get some help." He says the words so tenderly, I feel all protected and want to cry for some reason.

"I've been trying to tell her that," Lisa says brusquely, shattering my moment of bliss.

"The keys!" I bolt upright. "Where are the keys?"

"Are these what you're talking about?" Mitch lifts the man's keys. "I thought maybe they were yours, so I picked them up."

I breathe a sigh of relief. "Thanks." I explain the whole ordeal to him. Once he's convinced I'm all right, Mitch returns the keys to the man, and my workday is soon over.

With the vertigo incident and dinner behind me, I head out on the bunny slope. I figure if I practice, I'll be able to tackle the big mountain one day. I'm determined to lick this vertigo problem if it kills me. And it just might.

"You're sure you want to try that, Gwen?" Mitch calls out when he sees me leaving with my skis.

"I have to keep practicing."

He smiles as though he's proud of me. Memories of Mitch's protective hand earlier today comes to mind. I have to shake that off so I don't say something stupid like, "How do you feel about a Vegas wedding? Canned music? Tonight?"

"I guess maybe now is a good time to practice. They're predicting no snow for the next week or so." A downer mood invades his voice. He runs a hand through his hair. "I don't know how I can run a ski resort without snow."

I stare at him. He's kidding, right? There's enough snow on this mountain to build a community of igloos. "I'm sure everything will be fine."

"Easy for you to say." He frowns.

Here we go again. "Look, Mitch, you need to let go of your worry. Deal with the problems as they come and trust the Lord to help you through them."

He turns a cold glare my way. "Oh, you know all about that, don't you, Gwen? It's not as though you don't have a few issues yourself to deal with."

Wait. When did this get to be about me? I've never burst a blood vessel before, but I'm thinking that could happen. "I can't help the vertigo. Lots of people have vertigo."

"It's not a physical issue. You said so yourself."

Doggone it, I knew those words would come back to haunt me. "And your point is?"

"My point is don't preach to me until you take a hard look at yourself. You know, 'he who is without sin cast the first stone'?"

I'm realizing I've had very few fun moments lately, and that's making me downright mad. "I was trying to make you feel better."

"With a cliché?"

"Why can't you see the positive side of *anything*?"

"Why can't you be realistic?"

"Face it, Mitch, you're a worrywart."

"Face it, Gwen, you live with your head in the clouds. No wonder you get sick."

A squeak escapes me, and I want to whack him upside the head with a snowball, but he turns on his heels and stomps away. I slam the door behind me and head for the bunny slope.

Shoving a piece of gum into my mouth, I chew the dickens out of it. It's a whole lot better than what I had in mind for Mitch Windsor.

Chapter Fifteen

Mitch pretty much makes himself scarce over the weekend. It's better that way. I don't have the patience for him right now. And I'm out of cashews. I'm just not happy when I'm out of cashews.

Despite the fact that Mitch is offering free skiing to people over fifty today, our business is fairly status quo. He's trying so hard to make the business work, but I suspect he's barely able to make payments at this stage.

A tall man with salt-and-pepper hair trudges into the shop, stomping snow from his boots. He pulls off his gloves and rubs his hands together as he walks up to the counter.

"Boy, it's cold out there. But a skier can't stay away from these resorts when you folks keep running all these specials." He digs his billfold out of his pocket.

I smile. "Yeah, Mr. Windsor does offer a lot of specials," I say, bragging on Mitch even though he is a worrywart.

"He's not the only one. That place down the road does, too. Dream Slopes something or other. They're offering the same thing, free skiing to everyone over fifty today. I went there this morning. Thought I'd check this out this afternoon." He thumbs through his wallet for the right bills.

Monica has done it again. I glance at Lisa. She makes a face and shrugs. How is Monica finding out about Mitch's plans? He has to be telling her. Is she drugging him or what? Delilah with scissors? He did get his hair cut recently. Now, I'm no Angela Lansbury, but I want to know what's going on around here.

Lisa makes the man his cappuccino while I take his money. Afterward, he heads over to a table. Lisa and I talk quietly behind the counter.

"How do you think Monica is finding out about Mitch's business plans?" Lisa asks, stirring the whipped cream in her chai tea.

"I have no idea, but I want to find out."

"You going sleuthing again?"

I frown. "I just want to help Mitch."

"You like him, don't you?" Lisa studies my face.

"Yes—no—I don't know." Though I consider

Lisa a good friend, I don't want to talk about it. Besides, his moodiness is getting on my nerves.

She throws me a look that tells me she doesn't believe me. I don't say anything.

"Well, good luck. I've yet to see him settle down with anyone. I mean, if Monica can't snag him—"

Her words hit me between the eyes. One look at me and she stops short.

"What were you going to say, Lisa? Go ahead and finish."

"Oh, nothing. Doesn't matter."

"You were going to say if Monica can't snag him, no one can, right?"

"Well—"

"Don't worry about it. I'm sure you're right." I lift my chin a notch. "I'm not out for the 'Mrs.' title. I have plans of my own." I try to sound convincing. Neither of us is buying it.

"Of course not. You'd rather have the 'Barista' title for the rest of your life, right?"

"Ri— What?"

Lisa smiles at me, and I see she has me cornered. Tumbleweed is calling my name. In fact, I'm beginning to wonder about Herbert Caudell, and that just scares me.

The door creaks open, and Mitch walks inside. He pulls off his hat and shakes the snow from it.

With heavy steps, he walks across the floor. "Hi, Gwen. I'll take a mocha with whipped cream."

Uh-oh, he wants less caffeine. This can't be good. "One mocha it is."

I scribble some notes on the cup for Lisa and hand it to her. I drum my fingers on the counter. "I'm sure glad it's snowing." I'm trying to encourage him, but nerves make me look away.

"Won't last. Only a few flurries."

My gaze collides with his, then I try to act as though his complaining isn't bothering me. "Business looks pretty good out there. It took a while for me to get on the ski lift today." I'm struggling to find something positive.

"It's been better." His words remind me of pruning scissors, snipping off any extra detail, leaving only what is absolutely necessary.

Fine. He doesn't want encouragement right now. He wants to linger in self-pity. So let him. I don't have time to babysit.

I walk into the back room. I'm tired of these conversations. He worries and complains, and I have no use for that. I've tried to encourage him the best way I know how, but nothing seems to work. He is bent on seeing things in the worst light possible.

I pull some bottled flavorings from a box and prepare to store some on our shelves.

"Gwen." I turn around to see Mitch standing in the doorway.

"Yes?"

"Listen, you're right. Once again, I'm—" He stops when he sees my face. "I'm sorry." He turns and walks out of the room. I stare after him. Maybe I'm only beginning to see the kind of pressure he's under to make this business work.

The flurries are still falling when I leave the coffee shop later. I pull the door tight and lock it. I step onto the carpet of white and lift my face toward the sky. I'm actually getting into this cold weather. The chill invigorates my spirit and, these days, that says a lot. Opening my mouth, I let a snowflake fall on my tongue. Not the most mature thing I've ever done, but there you are.

"You actually eat that stuff?" Mitch steps up beside me.

"Didn't you ever eat fresh snow with a splash of vanilla as a kid?"

"Um, no. How did you eat snow in Arizona?"

"When I was a kid, we used to visit my aunt and uncle in Indiana, and they had plenty of snow." We tromp through the snow toward the ski lift.

"You really enjoy everything, don't you?" Mitch asks.

"I try to."

He shakes his head. "Wish I were more that way."

That makes two of us.

"My sister gave me a good talking-to this afternoon."

"Candace called?"

He nods. "She said she'll call back tonight so she can talk to you."

That makes me feel better. After all, she and Lauren got me into this mess.

"You're really good friends, aren't you?"

"Yeah, we are."

"Women are lucky that way."

"What way?"

"Oh, I don't know. You know how to make friends and keep them. Guys don't really make friends as easily. I mean, when we hang out, we only chat—work stuff, repairs, that type of thing. Women go deeper. That's hard for us."

Well, there's a news flash.

"At least that's been my experience."

We slip onto the ski lift and head down the mountain. I still hate these things. The metal creaks and groans in the wind, convincing me the lift could give out any moment.

I'm surprised that Mitch is opening up with me. I haven't figured him out yet. One minute he charms my socks off; the next minute, I want to whack some sense into him.

The lift manages to carry us to the bottom of

the slope, and we slip off. I breathe a prayer of thanks.

"So, Gwen, you've been here for several weeks now. Want to tell me what you think of the place?"

"I think it's great."

We keep walking and from my peripheral vision I can see him looking at me. "What, do you find that so hard to believe?"

"Well, you did tell me you don't like cold weather."

"That's true enough," I say with a laugh. "But I'm adapting."

"Like your iguana?"

"Something like that." I figure it's better to keep Guacamole out of this.

"I think Granny might be ready for some help in the kitchen. If it comes to that, would you be willing to switch over, or do you want to stay at Cool Beanz?"

My stomach sinks a little. After all, Lisa and I have gotten to be good friends, and I will really miss working with her. Granny had started warming up to me, but I didn't envision working with her anytime soon. Still, I confess that I do care about her. There's something, I don't know, endearing about her. I wonder how hard she will be to work with. "I'll go wherever you need me," I say, meaning it.

He stops, which causes me to pause and turn to him.

"I don't know how you put up with me and my moods. Honestly, I'm not normally moody by nature. But this place—well, you're a wonder, Gwen, that's all." His gaze spears my heart again, and do I even need to mention what's happening to my toes right about now?

"Thanks."

"No, thank *you*." With our eyes locked, his hands touch my shoulders and every nerve in me wakes up. He bends his head toward me. The scent of pine swirls around us, and I almost think I'm appearing in a cleaning commercial. Almost. The closer he gets, the harder my heart slams into my chest. He pulls me into his arms against a backdrop of frothy white mountains. Our lips are a whisper apart when…

"Well, Granny said I could find you here, and she was right. Though I seem to always be interrupting you two from something or other." Monica's voice is stiff and cold.

I want to say, "Yes, you do. So knock it off."

"Monica, what brings you here?" Mitch matches her ice for ice.

I try not to celebrate.

She glares at me then turns to him. "I wanted to discuss a business matter with you." She looks at me again. "That is, if you're serious about making this place successful. Of course, if you're too busy…" She says that as though I'm holding him back from his dream, and I resent her comment.

She's dangled the carrot and now she half turns so Mitch will think she's leaving. I want to grab Mitch's arm so he won't pursue her, but he's not a toy to fight over.

Surprising us both, he merely stands there and watches after her. I can't let him lose out on a business deal because of me. I take a step toward the house. Mitch grabs my arm. "Please, don't leave," he whispers.

I gulp. His touch sends a jolt clear through me. My toes are curled and tingling. There's enough energy charging through me that I could go up the mountain without a ski lift. I'm not ready to do so, mind you, but I could all the same.

Monica takes five or six steps then turns back. She flips her hair behind her shoulders with an impatient jerk. Her not-so-soft features remind me of Lot's wife once she turns to a pillar of salt. The word granite comes to mind.

"Are you coming, Mitch? I won't ask again."

"Monica, I have plans tonight. I would be happy to meet with you in the morning."

Her expression flickers from smoldering to

controlled anger. She lifts a forced smile. "All right, Mitch. How about eight o'clock?"

"Eight o'clock will work," he says matter-of-factly.

"See you then."

She's suddenly all cookies and cream. Why do I feel as though she's curdling beneath the surface? I gulp as quietly as possible. Somehow I don't think we've heard the last from Monica.

Once she turns and walks away, Mitch looks at me and let's out the breath he was holding. "Whew." He's trying to slough it off, but I'm thinking he's as worried as I am. "Now, where were we?" He grins and slowly pulls me to him, his hazel eyes holding mine. Our lips melt together, and I lose all thought of Monica what's-her-name....

I practically float back to the house. Not sure exactly what is going on between Mitch and me, but whatever it is, I'm liking it.

Mitch opens the door for me. We go to our rooms and prepare for dinner. Guacamole seems unusually quiet when I arrive. I think he's getting tired of being cooped up. Maybe Mitch wouldn't mind if I walked him downstairs after dinner. There's no one around for him to scare, after all.

"Granny, those were the best beef and noodles

I've ever eaten," I say, thankful that my mother isn't here to witness it.

Granny stands an inch taller. "My husband used to love my beef and noodles."

"Granny's the best cook in the family," Mitch says, dropping a kiss on her head. He pulls on his coat. "I've got to run and get some batteries from the store. You need anything?"

I clear the table of dishes while Granny and Mitch discuss what supplies are needed. After loading the dishwasher, I head back into the dining room to ask Mitch if he minds if I walk Guacamole, but Mitch has already left.

Figuring there's no harm in walking him, I run upstairs while Granny whips up some brownies in the kitchen. I'm not really sure how a depressed iguana looks, but I'm thinking Guacamole could qualify. His get-up-and-go has got up and gone.

"Come on, boy, it's not as bad as all that." I snap on his leash and tug at it. At first he just stands there. He can be so stubborn. I open the door and tug again. The expression on his face says he can't believe this is happening. I can respect that. I mean, the last time he went out of this room, an old lady screamed while standing on a bed, and a man backed him into a corner.

"It's all right, Guacamole. You're not in trouble." I tug again. This time he follows me. We walk slowly around the main floor. I want to warn Granny that I've got him in here, but I figure she'll be busy for a while in the kitchen. She told me earlier she was making brownies with icing. That should take a little time.

When we saunter near the window, I look outside to see Mitch's car coming down the lane. Guacamole's leash pulls against my hand, and I look down to see he's circled a stand and gotten himself caught.

I sigh. "How do you get yourself into these messes?" I unclip the leash so I can untangle him, but when I do, Guacamole makes a beeline for the kitchen.

"What are you doing?" I yell after him. "Get back here, Guacamole!"

Mitch no sooner steps inside than a commotion comes from the kitchen. Pots banging, dishes crashing against the floor. Forget defense. Granny's taking charge. "You get yourself back here, you belly-crawling, green-eyed—"

"Guacamole!" I shriek when I see Granny raising the broom high above her head and aiming straight for Guacamole's swishing tail.

"Granny, no!" Mitch yells.

"I'll be switched if I'm gonna let some scaly, cold-hearted reptile crawl into my kitchen and take over." She runs after Guacamole as he scampers into the dining area, his swishing tail re-sembling a runaway caboose.

It takes a while, but Mitch finally gets Granny calmed down, and I get Guacamole back in my room. He's hibernating in a back corner, which lets me know he's plenty upset.

But he's not as upset as I am.

"I trusted you, and this is the thanks I get," I say, stomping around in my room. I know it sounds crazy for me to talk to him like this, but that reptile knows more than he's letting on.

I should have warned Granny, then she wouldn't have overreacted when she saw him. He took her by surprise, that's all. She was plenty mad, though. I'm not sure, but I think I heard her give Mitch an ultimatum. A fresh wave of anger hits me.

"You may just get us sent back to Tumbleweed." I start pacing. "Well never again, buster. You can just stay cooped up in this room till springtime for all I care!"

When I finally calm down, I leave my room to go check on Granny. I mean, I know Guacamole can be hard to take, but I think Granny is a bit harsh with him. I remember his swishing tail. Then again, maybe she's not.

No doubt she would love nothing more than getting rid of us. She's had it in for me from the start. I don't measure up to her expectations no matter what I do. And she overreacts as far as Guacamole is concerned. She purposely makes a big stink about it. Maybe she let Guacamole loose earlier so she could force me to go home. My heart hurts to think she could do that. I refuse to believe it. I'll just let the question hang out in the cosmos for now. I'll come back to it later.

Mitch meets me in the dining room. Granny is nowhere in sight.

"We need to talk, Gwen."

That familiar sinking feeling returns. If only I had some cashews.

Mitch points toward the sofa in the great room. I sit down and he sits beside me, not too close, but close enough that I get a whiff of his cologne, a musky, woodsy scent that makes me want to sit in front of a fire on a warm, fuzzy rug.

"We have a problem," he begins. I can tell he is measuring his words here, so I know he doesn't want to offend me. That has to be a good sign.

"Is it green, has a tail and crawls on the floor?"

"That's the one."

I don't know what to say. Love me, love my iguana? Something tells me that won't work. I stare at my fingers.

Mitch scoots closer. I wish he wouldn't do that. I can't think clearly when he's that close to me. I enjoy it, mind you, but I can't think.

"Listen, Gwen, I can't let Guacamole run free in this place."

"It's my fault. I shouldn't have brought him down to walk around. He needed a little exercise, and I thought the walk would do him good. But then his leash got all tangled with the stand when I looked out the window. I had to unleash him so I could pull the leash free, and, well, the rest of the story you know."

We sit in silence for a minute.

"It's not only tonight, but also the other times when he was caught outside of your room that bothers me."

His expression tells me I'm not going to like what he's about to say. I brace myself.

"We have to get a cage. One where he can't get out. He's no longer free to roam your room."

Why not just tell me my baby has to go to prison? I think Mitch sees the pain on my face.

"He'll be all right, Gwen. You have to understand my position."

"I do."

"Then you agree?"

With reluctance, I nod. At least he's not making me go home. Maybe Granny had a change of heart. Whatever the reason, I'm thankful. I'm not ready to leave whatever chance I have with Mitch here, for the sake of an iguana.

Now, don't get me wrong. I love Guacamole, I really do. But the bottom line is my exotic pet will not be there for me when I'm old and gray.

Guacamole is a comfort. Guacamole is a dip. I vote for a cage.

Just call me Benedict Arnold.

Chapter Sixteen

Mitch didn't make me go through the expense of buying a cage for Guacamole. A friend of his made one for us. It offers Guacamole plenty of room to roam, but the truth is he has been pouting since he got it.

Great. An iguana with attitude. I'm sure on some level this is payback for my teen years.

Well, I've decided to get to the root of my vertigo problem, so I signed up for the clinic that Lisa mentioned. I leave in the morning. I have no idea what to expect, and I admit that I'm a little nervous about it. Who knows what they'll find out when they go snooping around in my brain? It's a scary thought.

I offered to make taco salad for dinner, so I need to get downstairs. I've barely had time to get in the door from work, but such is life.

I busy myself in the kitchen, and Granny tells me she'll set the table. Before long we're both finished. The kitchen smells of spicy meat and salsa. I put everything in bowls and place them on a tray. Granny steps into the kitchen.

"I have a headache, Gwen. I'm going up to bed. If I get hungry, I'll come down and eat later. Right now, I couldn't eat a bite."

"Are you all right?" Granny doesn't exactly appear the picture of health on an average day. I'm thinking a good stiff wind could carry her into the next county.

"I'll be fine. I think I need a little nap." She starts to leave then swivels back to me. "Oh, and Mitch is washing up for dinner. Should be down in a minute." She winks and leaves before I can comment further.

I'm not sure what that's all about, but I hope she's feeling better soon. I have far too much food here for only Mitch and me.

With a quick puff, I blow hair from my eyes, pick up the tray and carry it into the dining room. Mitch enters the room at the same time. When I look at the table, I almost drop my tray.

"I—" The words stick in my throat.

Mitch whistles. "This is some spread, Gwen." Mitch sweeps his hand across the dinner table dressed with flickering candles, linen cloth, napkins, fancy plates and silverware. "All this for taco salad?" A teasing glint touches his eyes.

"Gr-Granny set the table." The words come from my mouth, but I still don't believe it.

Mitch looks as skeptical as I feel. "Granny did this?"

I nod.

"Where is Granny?" he asks.

"She went up to her room to rest for a little while. She had a headache."

A wide grin lights his face. "Granny did this." There's a sort of "Go Granny" tone to his voice here. His gaze goes from the table back to me. "Well, let's eat."

We sit down and our chairs knock against the hardwood floor as we scoot up to the table. Mitch reaches for my hand and sends a prayer heavenward. I try not to get excited about the hand-holding thing since we do that every mealtime, even with Granny. We soon start eating.

"This looks great, Gwen," Mitch says, scooping the seasoned meat into his taco shell. He passes the bowl of meat to me while layering on the salad fixings. "It's been a long day. I'm kind of glad we don't have any guests tonight. I can relax in the great room."

I smile. "You had an early morning, starting with your meeting with Monica. How did that go? Figure out how she knows our business plans?" I ask the questions innocently enough, but one look on Mitch's face tells me I've gone too far.

He blinks with surprise. His mouth tightens to a thin line. "I don't really want to talk about it."

There's an awkward moment. "I'm sorry, I didn't mean to pry. I was only meaning that—" I'm babbling, and I feel stupid.

His expression relaxes a little, but it's still somewhat guarded. Maybe he thinks I'm being too possessive, trying to smother him. Probably figures I'm ready to march him down the aisle. He should know I'm not that way. Well, okay, I *might* want to march him down the aisle, but I haven't bought the dress yet. The fact that I simply haven't found one that suits me has absolutely nothing to do with it.

"It's not your fault. It's me. I just don't know what to think about anything anymore." He puts his fork down and stares blankly in the distance.

"What do you mean?"

"It's hard to know who to trust."

"You know you can trust me, Mitch. Right? You know that?" I'm half afraid to hear his answer. I'm shocked that he could entertain the idea that I might have something to do with hurting his business.

He continues to stare at me. "I hope I can."

"But you've said yourself that Monica—"

"Monica can be sneaky, but we have been friends for a long time. I don't trust her, I know she's always snooping around for things that are none of her business, but I think she's more concerned with gaining my affections. I don't think even she would try to put me out of business."

"But *I* would?"

"I'm not saying that, Gwen." His voice sounds tired, defeated. "Sometimes Monica drives me crazy, but I meet with her because, well, she's teaching me—"

Wait. Could you spare me the gory details, please?

"About the business."

Uh-huh, and I have a diamond mine I'm trying to sell.

"What?"

"What, what?"

"You have that look on your face."

"I don't know what you mean, Mitch."

"You act as though you think I'm making this up."

"Why would I think that?"

"I don't know, why would you?"

I put my fork down. "Well, one minute you don't want Monica anywhere near this place, you act as though she's your archenemy, and the next minute you're telling me what a great friend she is. So which is it?"

He steels his jaw. "What is this, twenty questions? I'm not sure a couple of shared kisses entitles you to that."

I am speechless. Totally speechless. Well, maybe not totally. "I couldn't care less about that." I try to sound in control, but instead my voice squeaks. Think of the mice in *Cinderella*.

He reaches for my hand, and I yank it away. "Look, I didn't mean that."

I refuse to let the tears through that are stinging my eyes.

He runs his hand through his hair. "I don't know what to think anymore."

"That makes two of us." I'm starting to lose my appetite. This is serious.

His jaw clenches. "I don't get why you don't want me to talk to her."

"Listen, Mitch, I don't care if you talk to the Mona Lisa. I was merely making small talk. You seemed upset by Monica's presence last night, I thought—I don't know what I thought." Our eyes lock. I take the linen napkin from my lap and put it on the table. "I'm not hungry."

I get up and storm from the room. He deserves Monica Howell.

I close my door and throw myself onto the bed. I'm glad I'm leaving for the clinic tomorrow. I want to get away from this place, from Mitch and his precious Monica.

My phone rings. "Hello?"

"Hey, Gwen, it's Candace."

My heart sinks. I don't especially want to talk to her right now.

"What's wrong, is this a bad time?"

"Not the greatest."

"That's not the happy girl I know. Spill it."

Do I want to talk to her about her brother? Her only brother? The brother she is close to? Um, no.

"It's Mitch, isn't it?"

Silence.

"Gwen, what did he do? Do I need to hurt him?"

This makes me chuckle, because Mitch could wrestle a bear and win.

"That's better. Now talk."

"I don't know what's going on with him, Candace." I explain the whole thing about Monica, and how he seems wishy-washy where she's concerned. "He gets all mad at her, then the next minute he's defending her. What's that about?" A thought stabs the center of my heart. "Do you think he's in love with her?" I search the stand drawer for any stray cashews that might have spilled from my container. Nothing. Not even a crumb. Just when I thought the day couldn't get any worse.

"No way."

"How can you be so sure?"

"Because I know my brother. Look, Gwen, I know that Mitch would be mad if I told you this, but he's really confused right now. He thinks that someone is trying to ruin him. At first he met with Monica to learn some things about running a ski resort. Of course, she was all too eager to help him. Then suddenly she's beating him to the punch on discounts and business strategies. He wants to get to the bottom of how she knows these things."

"He suspects me."

"I know. But he doesn't want to. He cares about you, Gwen. Really cares."

"He has a funny way of showing it."

"Think about it. He hasn't known you all that long. He's not sure who to trust."

"It seems like a no-brainer to me, given Monica's past history with him, how she'll do anything to get him for herself. Now all of a sudden he's defending her."

"To you. While he sorts everything out. Look, if it helps at all, he's not defending her to me." I hear Candace sigh. "I don't want to betray my brother's confidence, but I want you to know where he's coming from."

My spirits sag. I don't want to make Candace

betray Mitch's trust. "Don't say any more. I'm not trying to pit you against Mitch. I'm confused, that's all."

"I understand. But don't give up on him yet, Gwen. He needs you."

"Yeah, right."

"Trust me. He does."

We talk a little longer. I tell her about my appointment with the clinic, Granny's beautiful dinner table and Guacamole's latest antics.

"Don't you worry, Gwen. Things are going to be all right. You'll see. I've been praying, and I know God will see you through this."

"Yeah, well, I wish He'd let me in on what's happening," I say drily.

Candace laughs. "Don't we all? You take care of yourself. Don't make any hasty decisions. Call me if you're unsure about anything, all right?"

"Yeah." I'm hesitant here, but also feeling a little better now that I've talked with Candace.

"Keep praying."

"I will."

We say our goodbyes, and I'm starting to think I might make it through this. Without another thought, I slip to my knees beside my bed and pray. I've been trying to handle this thing on my own, and now my emotions are involved. I need the Lord to guide me. Maybe I shouldn't have come here. I didn't actually seek His advice before moving, but it's a little late to ask Him about it now. So I'll see where He leads me from here.

After I finish praying, I realize I need to remind Mitch about my leaving for the clinic in the morning, in case he's forgotten. I probably won't have a chance to see him before I go. I don't really want to go downstairs and face him again, but I know it's the right thing to do.

I wash my face, refresh my makeup and head downstairs. Though they can't see me, I hear Mitch and Granny talking.

"I don't know what to think. I've had more complaints about her coffee. Why is that? She started out so well, now they're saying the coffee is bad. We're losing customers. I can't afford that, Granny."

"How do you know she's the one making the coffee? Don't those girls take turns?"

"Yes, but the customers describe Gwen as the one who made it."

"You told me she made good coffee," Granny persists.

"She always has—up to now."

"It doesn't make sense," Granny says.

"I know." Mitch's voice sounds tired.

"Now listen, Mitch. Just because you've been betrayed in the past, there's no call for you being overly suspicious now. Innocent until proven guilty, remember?"

"Don't forget that Candace and Lauren talked her into this job. With her parents traveling six months out of the year, Candace and Lauren were afraid Gwen would shrivel up in her small town. They were looking out for her, but I'm wondering if they know her as well as they think. I don't know, maybe Gwen wants to go home. If my business goes under, she wouldn't appear a failure. You know, she tried, but her employer lost his business routine." Mitch sighs.

"That doesn't sound at all like Gwen. She would *ruin* you so she could go home? I don't get it," Granny says.

"Yeah, I guess you're right. I just don't know what to think."

My stomach coils. I can't bear to hear any more, so I head back to the stairway.

What am I doing wrong? Have I not been paying attention? Maybe my mind has been on Mitch and not my work lately. I can't imagine what I'm doing, but I suppose it's possible that I'm messing things up. I can't seem to do anything right these days. My hand grabs the banister as I take the first step. A splinter beneath the banister pierces my finger.

"Gwen?"

I turn.

"Did you need something?" Mitch stands there looking as handsome as ever, and I want to cry. Whether from the splinter, from the evening, from his appearance, I don't know.

"Um, I wanted to remind you that I'll be leaving in the morning for the clinic. Lisa is all set to work, and our temporary gal is in place to cover for me as well."

"Thanks." Mitch steps closer to me. "Listen, Gwen—"

I step back. "I really need to get packed for my trip."

He nods, keeping his gaze on me. "I hope they can help you."

"Thanks," I say, though I'm not sure anyone can help me at this point. I continue up the stairs, the splinter causing my finger to throb. I don't know which hurts more, my finger or my heart.

I'm thinking my heart.

Chapter Seventeen

Since I was at the clinic, I haven't seen Mitch all weekend, and somehow I managed to get through breakfast and up to Cool Beanz without running into him, which is just as well. I've had enough emotional upheaval over the weekend to last me a while. The clinic, I believe, was a success, but I suppose the proof will be in whether I can look down without my world spinning out of control. What am I saying? It's already out of control without me looking down.

The last customer walks out the door.

"I'm going to take a break before the lunch crowd hits, want to join me?" Lisa asks.

"Sure."

We grab our coffees and head for a table.

"So, you going to tell me what you found out this weekend, or is it too personal?"

"No, I can tell you. It's the strangest thing. I would never have remembered the problem, had I not gone to the clinic."

Lisa leans into the table, no doubt eager to hear what I've found out. Right then the door opens, and Mitch walks inside. The sight of him causes my heart to pause.

"Can a guy get an Americano?"

I jump up. I'd rather do that than be at the table alone with him. "I'll get it."

"Thanks."

I watch Lisa and Mitch talk while I prepare his Americano. Grabbing a napkin, I take his hot drink to him.

"Thanks."

Mitch has dark circles under his eyes. Must have had a busy weekend.

"So, Lisa tells me you were getting ready to talk about your time at the clinic. Is it all right if I listen in, or do you want me to leave?" A look of apprehension covers his face, and I can tell he thinks I don't want him around.

"You can stay," I say with a guarded heart. I'm not ready to let down my defenses. I'm still stinging from his suspicions.

"Long story short is this—when I was about four years old, I rode the Ferris wheel with my dad. Once we approached the top of the wheel, the ride stopped. I looked down and saw some people lift a man from his seat. He was limp, and they carried him away on a stretcher. I think he died. Somehow in my childish brain I put two and two together and reasoned that if you look down, bad things will happen."

"Wow," Mitch says. "It's amazing how things can affect little kids." He takes a drink of coffee. "Hey, this is good," he says, like he's pleasantly surprised.

"Do you think you're cured now, Gwen?" Lisa wants to know.

"They say I am, but I won't know until I actually put it to the test."

"Are you going to do that?" Lisa seems totally devoid of compassion. She seems more of a sensationalist. I get the feeling she doesn't care what this puts me through but wants to see how I handle it. Must be all those reality programs—sort of desensitizes us.

"I don't think I'm ready yet. I need time to work through this."

"I think you're right," Mitch says in my defense. I smile my thanks.

"So do you think I should go on the Dr. Phil show?" I ask with a laugh.

"Sounds to me like you've already got it licked." Mitch drains the last of his Americano.

Two couples walk through the door. "There she

is," one of the men says, pointing to Lisa. "Would you mind making our drinks for us? We came in here over the weekend, and you make the best coffee we've ever had."

Lisa grins. "Sure, be happy to." She glances at Mitch, then to me. My throat feels tight. Why doesn't someone paint a big *L* for loser across my forehead?

"Well, I'd better get back out there." Mitch stands, throws his cup away and heads for the door. Right before he leaves he turns back around. "Great coffee, Gwen."

I can't help wondering if he's saying that to make me feel better or to convince himself that I'm not out to hurt his business.

He smiles once more then leaves. I try to push it back in place, but I feel my guard slipping. If only he didn't have a smile that could make my scalp tingle.

Passing the customers, I smile. They have no idea what turmoil they've caused me by paying Lisa that compliment in front of my boss.

I collect their money while Lisa makes the drinks. Once they are seated, I clean the counter.

I turn to see Lisa staring at me. "What?"

She picks up her cup. "I see how you look at him."

"Who?"

"Mitch, that's who."

I laugh. "What brought that on?"

"I was thinking about it while I made the drinks. I don't want you getting hurt, Gwen."

Here we go again. "What do you mean by that?" I clean the spigot on the cappuccino machine.

"Well, he's been spending a lot of time with Monica."

I stop and turn to her. "How do you know that?"

"I see them around town."

I feel my chin lift a notch and go back to cleaning. "Well, she's helping him with the business."

I glance up in time to see a patronizing smile touch her lips. "Oh, trust me, they weren't talking business when I saw them."

Acid coats my stomach. I shrug. "It's none of my business what they're talking about." I rinse out the cloth.

"Are you saying you don't care about Mitch in that way?" she persists.

"What way?" I act totally oblivious to her insinuations.

She steps up to me. "Come on, Gwen. You know you like him. A lot."

I shut off the water, wring the cloth and turn to her. "He's a good friend," I insist. I mean, Lisa is a friend and all, but I'm still not ready to share my innermost secrets with her.

She glares at me. "Suit yourself. But don't blame me if he hurts you. I've told you before he leaves a trail of broken hearts wherever he goes."

For some reason, I can't help thinking there's more to this discussion than she's telling me.

"Monica's been after him for years. And to be honest, Gwen, he's taking notice."

Excuse me, I don't want to hear this anymore. "You know, I think I'll finish the inventory in back. You cover out here, and if we get too many customers, let me know, and I'll come back and help." Before she has a chance to answer, I leave. I've had all the advice I can handle for a while.

"Granny, I'm going to the store. Do you need anything?" I poke my head into the kitchen and smile. I still haven't figured out why she set such an elaborate dinner table for taco salads the other night.

Granny's wiping off the stove. She stops, puts her hand on her hip and thinks a moment. "Now that you mention it, I could use a gallon of milk," she says. "Let's see, I think Kaci needs some more glass cleaner, too. That should do it." She reaches into her pocket and pulls out some money and gives it to me. "Thanks."

"No problem," I say. "Be back in a jiff." I head

out the door and off to the local grocery. The weather has been wonderful the past several days. Of course, Mitch doesn't think so. It's not snowing. He's not happy unless we have precipitation of some kind or other. Guess a honeymoon in Hawaii is out. That thought almost brings my heart to a halt. Like there's a honeymoon on the horizon with Mitch Windsor. According to Lisa, that privilege will go to Monica Howell. Well, at least their wedding gift is easy. Since poison is out, monogrammed towels will have to do.

By the time I get to the store, my mood is drooping. I don't want to think about Mitch being with Monica. I've come to face the truth. I have fallen in love with Mitch Windsor. Is that possible after only, what, six weeks or so? I think I believe in love at first sight. But there's more to him than meets the eye. That's what I love about him. He's not only handsome, but he's a lot of other things I admire in a man.

Oh, why didn't I stay in Tumbleweed where I belong?

I yank a cart free from the others and head toward the produce section. Mitch is obviously more attracted to Monica than he lets on. Otherwise, he wouldn't bother to spend so much time with her. I know Candace doesn't think so, but I don't think she knows everything there is to know about her brother. It doesn't take that many meetings to get a business up and running. Besides, who works with their competitor on business matters? It's ridiculous.

"Well, well, if it isn't Gwen Sandler." The sneer in the voice makes the hairs on the back of my neck bristle. I turn around.

"Hello, Monica."

She picks up a head of lettuce and checks it over. "So, Mitch tells me you think you've kicked the vertigo problem."

He's talked to her about my vertigo? Now that just bothers me. A lot. I mean, that's personal. Why would they be discussing me, anyway?

"Time will tell, I guess." I have no intention of talking over this problem with her.

"I imagine it's tough to have a problem with vertigo and work on a mountain."

"I get by."

"Do you miss your teaching job?"

He told her that, too? It's a good thing I didn't give him my social security number or she could steal my identity. Not that she would want to or anything.

"I miss the kids, not the work."

She rummages through the heads of lettuce. "Do you plan to return any time soon?" She acts disinterested, but I know she's holding her breath until I give my answer. I think I'll dangle a carrot just out of reach, give her enough information to make her salivate.

"Oh, I don't know. I haven't really decided yet. I kind of like it here." I pick up a lettuce head and pretend to examine it.

"Mitch is wonderful, isn't he?"

I turn to her with a start. "What?"

Her eyes narrow. "Oh, don't act so surprised. I've seen you two together, remember?"

"Well, I—"

Monica gives a tight little laugh. "Don't let it worry you. He has that effect on almost everyone." She takes a deep breath and blows out a long sigh. "Still, he can be a player." She puts the lettuce back in the bin. "But even knowing that, I enjoy my time with Mitch. Why, when we went out the other night—"

Excuse me?

"Well, let me say only that Mitch knows how to treat a woman."

The head of lettuce falls out of my hands and thumps to the floor. There's a slight slope, so the lettuce journeys across the aisle, looking like a runaway head. I see Monica's face on the green leaves and have to blink. Hard. A lady barely dodges it with her cart. It pongs off the edge of a display, rolls a little farther and finally stops at the feet of a young man who is putting stickers on the produce. He looks up at me and smiles.

Monica makes a face at my blunder. With a hike in my chin, I saunter over to retrieve my lettuce with all the dignity of the Bachelorette at a rose ceremony.

"Well, I guess I'd better let you get back to your shopping. So nice to see you again." Her voice tells me she doesn't mean that in the least. "Say, will you tell Mitch about tomorrow night—oh, never mind. I'll tell him when he calls me. Ta-ta." She waves and practically glides down the aisle. I notice produce boy is drooling after her, and I want to wallop the little twerp with my head of lettuce.

I shove my cart ahead and walk past him, giving him a sharp glare. Though he's clueless, it makes me feel better.

Once I collect Granny's items and a new can of cashews, I head back to the B and B. I can't make sense of all this. Is Mitch actually dating Monica? Why would he say all those things to me about her if he had feelings for her? I stop my car at a traffic light. Not that he owes me an explanation. I shift in my seat, straightening, sitting taller. On second thought, the fact that he's kissed me makes him owe me *something*.

By the time I stumble into the house with the groceries, I've worked myself up to a good snit.

I'm thinking Mitch is using Monica and me, which would be consistent with his "player" reputation. All that gibberish about how he's changed, well, I'm not so sure I believe it anymore.

I dump the groceries on the counter and proceed to put things away in a huff.

Mitch walks into the room. "I heard someone come in and by the sound of things, I thought he was destroying our kitchen." He laughs.

My confetti is put away for the night, thank you very much. No party here. I keep putting away the groceries.

"Granny went on to bed. She had a headache." Mitch steps up beside me, grabs the milk and carries it to the fridge.

"I'm sorry she's not feeling well."

He comes over and puts his hand on my arm. "Hey, you doing all right?"

I steel myself to his touch. Raising my eyebrows I say, "I'm fine, why?" I defy him to melt my resolve tonight.

"Just wondering. By the way, I meant to tell you how nice you look in that yellow sweater."

"Thanks." Cold. I sound completely cold.

He keeps his hand on my arm. "I'm glad you're getting that vertigo thing under control, too."

"Mmm-hmm."

"Listen, Gwen, about what I said the other night, you know, about the kisses not entitling you to—"

"Don't worry about it," I quip and pull away. "See you in the morning," I call over my shoulder and head for my room. My heart feels as heavy as my steps. I don't want to treat him that way. It doesn't matter what he's said to me. I don't like to hurt people, and though he may not be in love with me, I think I've hurt him.

I reach the top of the stairs when a knock sounds at the front door below. I step inside my room but peek through a sliver of opening. It's Monica. What is she doing coming over at eight o'clock at night?

I suddenly feel the need to get a drink of water.

By the time I'm downstairs, Monica and Mitch are already comfortable on the sofa. I wave and head for the kitchen, keeping an ear toward their conversation. My mother would have a fit.

I can't make out what they're saying but I think Monica mentioned she's picking up a bag that he has of hers. Oh brother. She'll make up any old excuse to see him.

I fuss around in the kitchen a moment so they won't get suspicious of me listening in. Would they think I'm that kind of person? Of course they would. I grab a glass of water and without so much as taking a sip, I place it on the counter.

Okay, so I peek around the corner to watch them and strain my ears to try to hear what they're saying. Monica's back is to me, but I can see Mitch. He's all smiles as her perfectly manicured hands wave delicately about while she talks. Her soft voice reeks of femininity. I just wish I could hear what she was saying. Before I have time to get bitter about Miss Perfect, I see a movement near her bag at the side of the sofa.

Now I have no idea what's in her bag, but it's big, it's open and it's on the floor. What I see standing a few inches in front of her bag causes my blood to freeze in place. It's the scaly head of one beady-eyed reptile. How did he get out of his cage this time?

My gaze shoots to Mitch and Miss Perfect, who haven't noticed the intrusion on their happy conversation. Though the idea of Monica spotting Guacamole has its merits, I don't even want to think about Mitch's reaction. There must be something I can do to keep them in blessed ignorance, but what? If I step into view, Mitch will see me. If I say anything, they both might hear me.

I glance around the kitchen. Quickly, I tiptoe over to the refrigerator and pull out some fresh green beans. Since I only need a few to lure Guacamole away from his mission, Granny shouldn't miss them.

By the time I look back at Guacamole, he has inched toward Monica's bag. His head faces my way, then dips into the bag. I gulp. Monica and Mitch continue talking while I scrunch down near the kitchen opening. I'm hoping I'm too low for Mitch to see me as I wave the green beans in my hand.

Suddenly, Guacamole's head once again comes into view. I breathe a sigh of relief and wave the green beans with a furry. Guacamole looks up—and I *know* he sees me—then ignoring me, he sticks his head right back into the bag. Granny won't have to make him into a purse, I will!

Soon the bag widens, bulges to his shape, then freezes. That can only mean one thing. Guacamole has found a warm resting place.

We are so busted.

"Let me get you a drink," Mitch says, standing.

Monica says something and Mitch heads my way. Panic slices through me. I drop the green beans and rush to grab my glass of water.

"Gwen, I thought you had gone back to your room already," Mitch says, surprise on his face.

My hand goes to my neck, "Oh, I was still thirsty," I say with a grin. My glass of water is shaking, so I grab hold with both hands.

"Everything all right?"

I've seen that look of suspicion on his face before. He knows something's up.

"Fine," I say, producing my best smile. My heart is pounding the daylights out of my chest, and I take another drink of water, praying I don't choke.

A scream slashes the silence. My eyes feel like they're going to pop out of my head. Mitch's eyes narrow at me a millisecond before we both bolt for the great room.

"Get that—that thing out of here!" Monica wails. I'm pretty sure the windows rattle here.

With his swishing tail leading the way, Guacamole backs out of the bag. Poor thing probably doesn't know what hit him. She's got him plenty mad.

"I'm sorry, Monica," I blubber, practically shoving the green beans in Guacamole's face.

"Oh, he's horrible," Monica says with a shiver. She goes over to Mitch, hides her face in her hands and leans against his shoulder.

Okay, now *I'm* mad. Doggone reptile.

By now Granny enters the room, fists tight on her hips. The last thing I need is a verbal thrashing from Granny.

Time to start packing.

After much effort, Guacamole pursues the green beans and follows me back to the room.

Monica's cries soften to a whimper. The little dear.

I lock Guacamole in his cage, but he doesn't care. He has his treat. Of course once his food is gone, he'll be plenty mad because he hates being cooped up in that cage. He'll thump and scratch around so I won't get any sleep tonight.

I hide out in my room and hope Mitch will forget everything by the time Monica goes home. I can't stand the thought of the two of them together downstairs in a quiet house.

"Thanks a lot," I say to Guacamole. "I sure would like to know how you're getting out of this room."

Sitting on the bed, I pout a moment, trying to figure out what to do next. I look over at the nightstand where I always keep my Bible, but it's not there. How odd.

I look down and notice a small corner peeking from under the bed covers. This is really strange. Wouldn't I remember if I had dropped it? Maybe I knocked it off and didn't realize it. That's a possibility. Still, I wonder.

Someone knocks at my door. Great. Wonder if I can get my job back at the Oasis until the school year is over? I glance around the room. I was even growing accustomed to the beige. Didn't like it, mind you, but I tolerated it. Guess it doesn't matter now.

I open the door. Mitch stands before me wearing the expression of a boss. His jaw is set, his eyes fixed, his mission obvious. I'm so going back to Tumbleweed.

"I need to talk to you, Gwen. Mind if I come in?"

Like I have a choice? "No, come on in."

I step away from the door, and he follows me inside.

"Didn't we agree that you would keep Guacamole in his cage so that we wouldn't have any more problems with him sneaking into the B and B?"

"Yes, we did."

"And did you do that?"

"Yes."

"How can you say that?"

"Because it's true."

"Gwen—" he walks over and checks out the cage his friend made for Guacamole "—you and I both know there is no way Guacamole can get out of this cage if you put him in there." Mitch rattles the door on it, proving that it's snug.

"I know that."

Mitch gapes at me. "That's it? That's all you're going to say?"

"What more can I say? You wouldn't believe me anyway." My words are barely a whisper. I'm exhausted and tired of defending myself.

He steps closer to me. "Try me." His expression

tells me I had better come up with a solution, or I'll be having coffee with Herbert Caudell by nightfall tomorrow.

"I believe someone is letting him loose."

He stares at me. "Someone."

I nod slightly.

"And do you have any idea who that someone may be?"

His patience is growing thin. I can feel it.

"I don't know for sure."

"Great."

"But I have a suspicion."

"All right, let's hear it."

"I can't believe I'm even saying this. I like Granny, I really do. But let's face it, from the very start she hasn't exactly welcomed me with open arms. And, well, I think it might be her."

My door is still open when Granny walks up to it. "Mitch, Monica is ready to leave."

Granny's gaze collides with my own, and a cold chill sweeps across the room. Something tells me the temperature on Windsor Mountain is dropping.

Chapter Eighteen

Sunlight streams into my bedroom, and I reluctantly open my eyes. Memories of last night replay in my mind, making me want to pull the covers over my head and stay in bed.

I wonder if Granny heard what I said about her to Mitch. Maybe I'm jumping too quickly. What if she isn't the one who is letting Guacamole out of his cage? There is no possible way Guacamole could get free on his own, but who else would do it? No one else has access to the rooms other than the housekeeper, and she would have no reason for setting him free. Would she? Guacamole may have wandered out once while she was cleaning. But every time? Somebody's stirring up trouble. I think I'll keep an eye on her.

I manage to get through the day without any major confrontations with Mitch or Granny. They both have been far too busy to notice me. I guess I won't be switching from Cool Beanz to the B and B kitchen anytime soon at this rate. Not that it matters. I'm thinking I'm lucky to be employed.

"I'll see you tomorrow," Lisa calls out as I'm shutting everything down.

"Have a good evening." I run mechanically through my nightly routine. I hear her yank the door closed, and I'm shrouded in the silence of an empty building. Outside the wind howls across the mountainside. I don't want to go back to the B and B. I'm thinking with any luck I'll get eaten up by a bear.

I prepare a mocha and amble across the room to a chair. Two sips into my drink, I reflect upon my life over the past weeks. Everything in my world has changed so drastically. My home has changed to a different state. Mom and Dad are no longer around. I've managed to survive outside of Tumbleweed, but at what cost? In less than two months, I have lost my heart to a man who sees me as nothing more than a nuisance who owns a pet iguana.

The good news is my vertigo is on the mend—I think. Of course, I can't really know for sure until I try it out. I sip my drink. I want to do that, but I'm not sure I'm brave enough yet. My thoughts turn to my skis, which are in the back room. I've left them there for Lisa to use and also in hopes that one day I would gain the nerve to ski down the slope. Is tonight the night? The crowd has thinned, so if I'm going to embarrass myself, at least there won't be a lot of people around.

I get up and walk in the back room, pick up my skis and bring them into the dining area. Maybe if I look at them long enough, it will give me courage to try the slope. Placing them in plain view against the wall, I sit back down and stare at them.

The door squeaks open, and I look up to see Mitch walk in. My heart catches.

"Hi, Mitch. Would you like something to drink?"

"No, you're closed. I saw the light on and thought I would check on you."

I appreciate that comment. Must mean he's worried about me or something. That's good, right?

"Do you have a minute to talk before we go down to the house?"

Uh-oh, here it comes. "Sure," I say, thinking now would be a good time to ski down the mountain.

I jump up. "I'll fix you an Americano—or do you want a mocha?" I want to suggest a hike across Europe, a project, say, boring a hole through the mountain with a toothpick, anything to keep his mind off what he came in here to say.

"Are you sure? Well, all right, I'll take a mocha."

Great. The man needs to calm himself. I'm

thinking bearskin rug in front of a crackling fireplace would be so much better than a mocha.

I quickly fix his drink, pray for wisdom and the talk that's awaiting me, and soon I join Mitch at the table.

He swishes his drink around gently, I suppose to cool it off. "I guess you know what I want to talk to you about."

A night at the movies? Dinner out? A raise? One look at his face tells me no. "I have a pretty good idea." I'm hoping he lets me wait until tomorrow to pack.

"I don't know how Guacamole is getting out of his cage, but I can't let you think that Granny is behind his escapes. She would never do anything like that."

"Look, Mitch, I'm not trying to discredit your grandmother in any way—"

"But you are."

"I don't mean to, really, I don't." I tread lightly because I know he is fiercely loyal to his family. "I just don't know anyone else who can get into my room—"

"I can get into your room."

I'm staring at my drink, and I stop and look up at him. "Are you saying that you're doing it?"

"No. I'm saying it's ridiculous to think I'm doing it or Granny's doing it. The fact that we can get into your room means nothing." He takes a drink from his cup.

"Then who?"

He stares at me. A little too long. Long enough for me to think he's blaming me. I answer his silent question with a question.

"Why would I let Guacamole out of his cage, Mitch?"

"You tell me."

My heart sinks to my toes. "You think I'm doing it." Sadness chokes my words.

Mitch puts his drink down and sighs. "No."

I look up at him. His gaze holds mine. "I don't think that, Gwen. You would have nothing to gain. Well, except that I know there is no love lost between you and Monica. Still, that doesn't explain the other times." He lifts a weak smile. Something in his voice tugs at my heart. I notice the shadows beneath his eyes. I want to relieve his concerns, make him feel better.

"I would never do that. Not even to Monica." It might cross my mind, but I would never do it.

Neither of us blinks. I'm thinking I'll start tearing up here pretty soon, but I don't want to turn away until he does. In fact, I don't want to turn away at all. Those hazel eyes hold me spellbound.

"Look, Gwen, I don't know what's going on. I merely want to get through it and move forward." Another drink.

Move forward as in me by your side? Move forward as in go on without you? I'm not sure what to say.

"The only other person who has access to your room is the housekeeper."

"Kaci Butler."

"Right."

"I thought of her. I thought perhaps she got busy cleaning and Guacamole sneaked out, but it seems unlikely that it would happen several times."

Mitch thinks a minute. "That's true. Still, it's possible. And right now, that's all we've got."

I give a half nod.

"Let's handle it this way. Let's make it a point to pop in and out of the B and B throughout the day, unannounced, especially during the time Kaci is there. That way if there is a problem, we can catch her."

I'm wondering how I can leave the coffee shop like that during working hours.

"Wait until things slow down at the shop, then ask Lisa to cover for you. Don't tell her why. Tell her I asked you to check on some things at the house from time to time. She doesn't need to know everything."

I think it's odd he's being so secretive, but then he is right. Though Lisa is my friend, that does not make her privy to Mitch's work strategies.

"All right."

He nods and finishes his drink.

"Mitch, thanks."

"For what?"

"For giving me a chance to prove my innocence."

"I'm curious, Gwen. What would make you think Granny was letting Guacamole out of his cage? I mean, do you think Granny wants you fired?"

I squirm a little here. "Well, she seems to always question me on things. Wants to know how I do this or that. I feel like I don't measure up in her eyes."

"Measure up to what?"

"That's just it. I don't know what she's measuring me up for. I suppose the kitchen position."

Mitch smiles here and a teasing spark fills his eyes.

"What?"

"I'm sorry, Gwen. It seems you've fallen prey to Granny's scrutiny. She constantly screens possible candidates for me."

I think about that a moment. I mean, sometimes Granny's nice to me, but she keeps her guard up. That can only mean one thing. I don't measure up. Monica comes to mind. I didn't think Granny was crazy about Monica, either, but maybe after seeing what a miserable candidate I was, Granny opted for Monica. After all, Mitch and Monica both love to ski and they have matching initials. I just can't compete with that. What do I have to offer? Good coffee—and it seems some question that.

"But don't worry about it. She does the same thing to any eligible woman within a fifty-mile radius."

And that's supposed to make me feel better?

Mitch runs his hand through his hair, and I notice his face appears a little pale.

"How are you doing?" I ask, wondering if he'll think I'm getting as bad as Granny.

He lifts a weak smile. "I'm really tired today. A quick jaunt down the mountain will get the blood pumping through my veins once again." He winks, and of course, that gets *my* blood pumping. His gaze travels to my skis. "You going to try it tonight?"

Um, no? I want to be brave and say yes, but it's not going to happen. "I don't think so," I say, feeling like a failure.

"You'll know when the time is right." He pats my hand in the same way he pats his Granny's.

"Well, we'd better get down to the B and B

before Granny starts to worry and fuss about dinner getting cold."

I nod. "I'll be there in a few minutes. I want to clean our table first."

"You want some help?"

"No." I wave my hand. "It's not that much. You go on ahead. I'll be right down."

We both stand. "Thanks for the mocha. It was really good." He smiles and trudges out the door in his ski boots. Beyond the window, I see him strapping on his skis. If only I could do that with such ease.

I sigh and take our cups over to the trash bin. Once I have everything cleaned up, I start to leave when I catch a glimpse of my skis. Adrenaline kicks my pulse up a notch. My teeth tug on my lower lip. Can I do this? Fear holds me still for a moment. I imagine the chill on my face, the exhilaration of a journey down the mountain. I hear my adventurous self urging me onward. Strike up the band! Assemble the choir! Gwen Sandler is, this very day, skiing down Mount Windsor!

I search my brain for a scripture of encouragement and suddenly, a quote from the book of Esther comes to me. "And if I perish. I perish."

That's *so* not the scripture I was going for.

Before I can change my mind, I grab the skis and head out the door. Once outside I step into my skis and hear them snap into place. The sharp wind stings my face, and I shiver into my ski coat. With a prayer in my heart, I make my way to the top of the slope, thinking I must be crazy to try this. I mean, God has enough to do without having to save me from this mountain, right? I'm thinking Esther's words are a sign.

I decide to take one more look out over the mountain before I take off my skis. I can stand a broad sweep of the view without the vertigo kicking in. My gaze spots movement about midway down the slope. I look closer. It's Mitch. He appears to be bent over and trying to keep himself from falling. Why doesn't he ski on down?

It's really cold today, and most everyone has gone home. The few remaining people are a ways from us. Carefully, so I won't fall, I step back from the top of the slope and dig in my pocket for my walkie-talkie. Mitch requires that we carry them so we have instant contact with one another at any time.

"Mitch, are you all right?" I ask through the speaker. I can't tell if he's trying to get to his radio or not. I wait. Then I hear static that lets me know he's trying to respond.

"Gwen. Sick. Get help."

Adrenaline is at an all-time high. I could go

down the mountain on the ski lift and call for help, but that would take too much time. If I go down the slope and get vertigo, then I'm of no good to him at all. Do I risk it? *God, please show me what to do.*

I signal the house. "Granny, are you there?" Time is wasting. I'm frightened for Mitch. I don't have time to wait on her. "Granny, if you're there, Mitch is in trouble. Please call for help."

I stuff the radio back in my pocket. *Lord, if I ever needed a miracle, it's now. I can't do this on my own. Please cover me with Your strength and courage.* I clutch my poles in a death grip, take a huge breath and kick off the slope. A scream roars in my ears and peals across the mountain, sending chills clear through me. I want to hurt the person who has made the blood freeze in my veins.

Until I realize that person is me.

Chapter Nineteen

I think my heart took off right after the scream. *God, please help me.* My legs wobble, and I struggle to maintain control. My body stays in position as I swoop downward. My arms shake—whether from fear or the cold, I'm not sure. Mitch's body looms closer and closer. Right now I'm more concerned about him than myself. That can only mean one thing.

God has come through.

Once I arrive near Mitch, I wedge my skis to a stop and inch my way closer. I decide to get on my bottom and scoot sideways toward him so I won't lose my balance. "Mitch, are you all right?"

Still in his skis, he's bent over, clutching his stomach. Right as he looks my way, he slouches against me. I drop my ski poles and my arms latch on to his waist. We go careening down the mountain with wild abandon. If the vertigo is going to kick in, I'm thinking now would be the time.

"Hang on, Mitch," I yell, but since he's passed out, I don't think he's hearing me. Besides that, if he were in his right mind, he would never trust me to get him down the mountain. Judging by the way we're spinning out of control, I'm guessing he would be right.

By the time we get to the bottom, I still have my equilibrium. Well, sort of—I mean, who wouldn't want to throw up after swirling down a mountain?

Once we're perfectly still, I sit there a moment to get my bearings. I hear footsteps thumping through the snow.

"Hang on, we're coming," someone calls out. My head turns toward the voices, and I see some guys coming our way. Rather than try to get up with Mitch's dead weight against me, I decide to wait until the cavalry arrives. I only hope Mitch is all right.

In no time, the men have placed Mitch on a stretcher and hauled him to a nearby ambulance. Granny stays with the guests at the inn, and I travel on to the hospital to see what's going on with Mitch.

I'm thankful the waiting room is empty when

I enter. TV noise and children scuttling about would make me nervous right now. Picking up a magazine, I try to browse through it to keep my mind occupied, but it's not working. I finally give up and put it back on the table with the others.

I lean my head against the wall behind me and close my eyes. This is the first moment I've had to catch my breath since Mitch got ill. Instead of feeling victorious over my healing from vertigo, I'm all knotted up with fear for Mitch. I mean, he has to be okay, right? Still, his face was so pale and the shadows—the signs of illness were all there. Why hadn't I realized that's what it was?

Not that I'm blaming myself. There's nothing I could have done anyway. It's just that I haven't made life any easier for him. He's had the strain of the new business and then Guacamole and I come along and make Mitch's life miserable.

Would life be easier on him if I left now, or will he need me now more than ever? What if his business fails? I know how important it is for him to make this work. *Now he's sick. What will happen from here, Lord?* I'm scared for Mitch.

Fear. It seems to be the driving force behind everything I do. Me, fear-driven? Unfortunately, it's time for me to face the facts. The answer is yes, I've allowed fear to rule my life. Vertigo, fear of leaving my safety bubble in Tumbleweed, fear of taking risks. The list goes on and on. Instead of trusting God and seeking His direction, I've been doing the safe thing, or doing what I want without ever once consulting Him.

I wouldn't be in this mess right now if I had consulted Him. By *mess* I'm not referring to being here at the hospital with Mitch. I'm talking about being in love with a man who seems interested in someone else—namely, Monica. The thought of going back to Tumbleweed would once have brought me joy; now the idea depresses me.

"Gwen Windsor?" A man with a white coat and pants enters the room. The stethoscope dangling around his neck tells me he's the doctor.

No point in correcting him about my name, so I stand and say nothing. He probably thinks I'm Mitch's wife or sister or something.

"With the HIPAA confidentiality laws in place, I'm not at liberty to tell you Mr. Windsor's condition until he fills out the necessary paperwork, but he asked me to have you come to his room."

"Me?" He probably meant Granny or even worse, Monica. That thought alone depresses me.

With a puzzled expression he stares at me. "You are Gwen Windsor, aren't you?"

"Well, actually, I'm Gwen Sandler."

He looks surprised. "That's odd. He called you Gwen Windsor. Anyway, he told me to see if you

were here and to ask you to come to his room."
He shrugs. "I suppose with all he's been through
today, he's a little confused."

I smile. Bring on the confusion, baby!

The doctor gives me direction to Mitch's room,
and I'm feeling more lighthearted until I realize
the doctor has given no indication whatsoever if
Mitch's condition is serious or not. That thought
almost stops me in my tracks. I arrive at his door
and pause to take a deep breath.

"Some people will do anything to get out of
work," I say, entering the room.

Mitch's face lights up, and my insides warm in
response. "Uh-oh, you're on to me."

My eyebrows raise, and I walk over to his bed.
"How are you feeling?" His lips are cracked and
his face pale. I'm almost afraid to hear his answer.

"I've been better. But Doc tells me I'll be fine.
I'm a little run-down, have a flu bug and I'm de-
hydrated, but it's nothing serious. They're keeping
me overnight to make sure I get some liquids
down me, then I get to go home tomorrow."

I struggle to swallow. I'm not sure why I want
to cry. Relief, maybe? "I'm so glad, Mitch."

"Thanks." He searches my face, and I feel my
cheeks flame. "I understand you risked life and
limb to save me?" His eyes are dancing here.

I smile. "I wouldn't say that."

"Seriously, Gwen, I know it wasn't easy for you to ski down that mountain. You did okay, though?"

I nod. "I'm thinking my vertigo days are over."

"That's awesome." His eyelids droop a little, and I can tell he's getting sleepy.

"Listen, I'm going to let you rest. I can pick you up tomorrow when they release you, if you want. Lisa is working, so she can cover for me."

"Sounds good." His eyes close for a second.

"Talk to you later," I say, already edging my way out the door.

"Gwen?"

I turn around.

"You think the business will make it?"

"I think it will make it, Mitch."

"Thanks." His eyes close.

As I walk down the hallway, I barely notice the dark-haired woman in the white nurse's uniform and thick-soled shoes. The squeak of the gurney wheels does little to draw my attention to the man being carted onto an elevator. An older man hooked up to tubes in a machine that he's pushing across the floor barely gets my glance.

My thoughts are with Mitch Windsor. With all he's been through today, the one thought that consumes him is whether his business will survive.

I want to help him, to do what I can to make the

business successful, but I run the coffee shop. What more can I do? I've given him suggestions that I thought might help, and he's pursued some of them. Not that I have all the answers, but I wonder what holds him back sometimes.

When I get back to the B and B, I'm bone tired. I tell Granny about Mitch's condition, and she seems to feel better knowing it's nothing more serious. We finish talking, and I start for my bedroom.

"Oh, Gwen, I forgot to tell you that Monica told me to have you call her the minute you get home."

"She's heard about Mitch?"

"Yeah."

"I'm surprised she didn't go to the hospital."

Granny shrugs and hands me a piece of paper with Monica's number on it. The last thing I want to do tonight is talk with Monica Howell, but it looks as though I have no choice.

Once I'm inside my room, I take my shoes off and plop on my bed. If I have to talk to Monica on the phone, the least I can do is get comfortable. I pick up the earpiece and punch in the numbers.

"Hello?"

"Monica, this is Gwen."

Pause.

"Gwen Sandler."

"Oh, yes, Gwen. How's Mitch doing?"

I explain what happened and what Mitch said the doctor told him.

"This is exactly what I've been telling him," Monica says.

"What do you mean?"

"He can't run a business single-handedly. I've been trying to get him to partner with me. It's the only way his business will survive."

A sharp pain hits my stomach. She wants him to go into business with her. Mitch would never do that, would he?

"I think this will clinch it for him. I know he wants to do it, but his pride holds him back. You know, he wants to prove himself. Still, it makes much more sense to join forces with me."

When she says that, I can almost hear Darth Vader asking Luke Skywalker to join the dark side.

"Anyone can see it's much easier to share the load of a business than do it alone."

"Well, his sister shares the ownership with him." I'm hoping I'm not saying anything that is confidential.

"Yes, she does, but is she here to help? No. He has to shoulder the responsibility of everything alone. She merely shares the wealth."

"Candace isn't like that." My face burns.

"I'm not saying Candace is like anything." I can picture Monica's chin lifted here. "I'm merely stating that Candace is not here to help Mitch. He's got a lot on his shoulders. I want to help him."

Sure, you do. Right over a cliff.

"Well, I won't keep you, Gwen. Thank you for helping Mitch today. He says you're a good worker."

A good worker? I'm picturing a thick-bodied mule here, and the vision isn't pretty.

"I'm sure he appreciated it. I know I do."

I didn't do it for you. Something tells me it's time to hang up. "I was glad to help Mitch."

"I really want him to see how I can help him with his business," she says with a sigh. "The thing is, I think Mitch is worried about going into business with someone he is romantically involved with."

"Romantically involved?" My tongue stumbles over the words.

"Oh, you didn't know?"

"Know what?"

"Mitch and I are practically engaged."

I will my tongue to move, but it sort of lies there, thick and unyielding.

Monica gives a soft laugh. "Oh, I guess you didn't know. Men are so funny that way. Not ready to tell the world they're taking the step toward matrimony."

"Well, congratulations."

"Thank you, Gwen." She almost sounds sincere.

"Of course, there's no set date yet, but it shouldn't be too long. We're both over eighteen, after all." Another laugh. "So as you can see, we will eventually be in business together anyway."

"If that's the case, what are you worried about?"

"I'm not worried." Definite mood change here. "I figure the sooner we join our businesses before he gets too far in over his head, the better."

I suppose what she says makes sense, but I can't get my mind wrapped around it.

"It's the right thing, Gwen," she says with all the authority of a school principal, which is enough to make me fall silent.

I never argue with the principal.

Never.

Not as a child, not as an adult.

She pauses here. Probably filing her fingernails. "Oh, and don't you worry, Gwen. I'll make sure you have a job in the snack bar or the kitchen."

I can feel my face flaming now. If I could jump through the phone, I would. "Thank you, Monica. I'd better go for now." If I keep talking, I might have to hurt you.

"All right. Talk to you soon. Goodbye."

I hang up and take several deep breaths to calm down. Guacamole scuttles across the bedroom floor. I wish I could let him loose in Monica's room.

Engaged. She said they were practically engaged. What about the trust issue he has with her? Was he just telling me that so he could flirt with me? Panic rises. He kissed me, for crying out loud. I remember Lisa's words about him being a player. His own sister had said the same thing. Though Candace is convinced all that changed once he became a Christian. Surely he wouldn't string me along if he was planning to marry Monica.

No, wait. Maybe he was checking out his true feelings for Monica by flirting with me. He wouldn't be the first guy to have a last-minute fling before settling down. Would he use me that way? He doesn't seem the type. Still, with his past history, it makes me wonder.

I'm tired of all these struggles. Maybe now would be a good time for me to leave. I'll wait until Mitch gets home and feeling better, then I'll head back to Tumbleweed. I tried to make this adventure work. It did help me to see that I can survive away from my safety net if I have to.

My heart aches. I pick Guacamole up and put him on the bed. I try to cuddle him, but he's not in the mood. He walks around, his feet kneading the comforter beneath him. "You had better be nice, or I'll trade you in for a poodle." I try to joke around, which usually puts me in a better frame of mind. But not this time.

I fall back on my pillow. Maybe Monica is right. Oh, I don't know about the joining forces thing, but Mitch has carried a heavy weight on his shoulders by taking on this business. The school-kids and even the stay-at-home moms are less than reliable at times. It seems he's always working two jobs on any given day to cover for someone else. Then if you add me to the mix, the botched coffee, Guacamole's antics, my klutzy ways, not to mention the whole fear of heights issue, well, he's had his hands full, that's all.

Maybe she is the answer to his problems.

With a sigh, I get up. Checking my door to make sure it's locked, I prepare for bed. While I'm in the shower, the last thing I need is for Guacamole to get loose. By the looks of the latest inn guest, one glance at Guacamole will send her to her Heavenly reward. I couldn't handle that right now.

One thing is for sure. I know that I love Mitch Windsor. If only he loved me, too.

Chapter Twenty

I wake up the next morning to blinding sunshine and have to cover my eyes with my hand. Normally, I would welcome the sight, but today my throbbing head won't allow me. A gust of wind rattles the windowpane as I stumble out of bed.

Barefooted, I shuffle into the bathroom and grab some pain reliever. The tile feels icy beneath my toes. Guacamole takes one look at me and turns the other way. I don't blame him. When I glance in the mirror a scary woman looks back at me. My hair resembles a used wool pad. My face is puffy, and my head aches from crying before I went to bed.

Turning on the cold water, I lift my cup to the faucet. I take two pain relievers and wash them down with the lukewarm water. I have to wonder if this is any indication of how my day will be. If so, I'm thinking going back to bed might be a good option. I saunter back into my room and sit on the bed.

Mitch comes home today. Home. His home, not mine. I wonder if he and Monica will live here when they get married or if they'll move to her place. Not that it matters to me one way or another. I'll be back in Tumbleweed. Only a hop, skip and jump from Polyester Man. And I'm going back to Tumbleweed, why?

Because I have no life.

I'm trying, but failing, to pull up the happy attitude. It's just not there. Not even a pack of gum can bring it on. I reach into my drawer, open the can of cashews, open my mouth and throw in a handful. Okay, I'm getting a spark of my perky self.

The phone blares beside me, which does wonders for my head. "Hello?"

"So, how's the woman who saved my life?" Mitch is obviously feeling better and sounding mighty fine.

"I didn't save your life," I say drily.

"Yes, you did. In fact, you risked your own to do it."

Bring on the gold medal. "I'll let you live in your delirium."

"Things are better that way." He gives a deep-throated laugh that causes my toes to curl once again. Careful, Gwen. He's taken, I tell myself. My guard reluctantly slips back into place.

"Has the doctor told you what time you can go home?"

"I haven't seen him yet, but the nurse told me he usually releases his patients around noon. That's why I'm calling, actually."

Great. It's not because he wanted to call me his hero or anything, he merely needs a ride. "Yeah?"

"Can you pick me up after lunch?"

"I can do that." I grab a pen and piece of paper and write down the time. I'll be counting the minutes until I can drive to the hospital and pick up Monica's fiancé. I sigh.

"Is something wrong? I don't want to inconvenience you, Gwen. I can call someone else, if you would rather—"

"No, that's fine. I'm happy to come and get you."

"You're sure?"

"I'm sure."

"No major problems there so far, right?"

"Well, considering it's only seven o'clock in the morning, I think we're in good shape."

"Is it that early? I'm sorry. I've been up for a while, and figured it was around nine o'clock."

"That's all right. I haven't slept all that well, anyway." Doggone it, I didn't mean to say that.

"What's wrong?"

"Oh, nothing."

"Have I done something?"

"No, of course not."

I wonder if I should congratulate him on his engagement, but since it's not official, I decide to wait.

"Well, I'll let you get ready for work. I'll see you after lunch."

"I'll see you then." I hang up the phone and head for the shower. Hopefully, the hot water will ease the increasing pain in my head.

The morning passes without incident, and shortly after lunch I enter Mitch's hospital room.

"Now, there's a welcome sight," he says with a grin. All right, I want to know what kind of drugs he's on and if he can stay on them.

"Well, someone is feeling better." I smile, though my heart aches beyond belief.

"I can't tell you how much better I feel. They put enough liquids in me to drown me, but somehow I survived." He winks and stands to walk out with me.

A thin older woman, dressed in a white uniform and cap, pads into the room with a patient chart in hand. "I'm sorry, Mr. Windsor, but we'll need to take you to the front door in a wheelchair. It's hospital policy."

I don't miss the fact that Mitch clenches his

fists at his side and his Adam's apple bobs in slow motion as he swallows hard. It's easy to tell that he isn't used to being incapacitated. To say he is uncomfortable is an understatement.

"I'm feeling fine. Do I have to go in a wheelchair?" He turns his charm onto the nurse, but the pinch in her lips, the hike of her nose and her stiff posture all suggest he's wasting his breath. "Hospital policy," she quips. Quickly she makes a note on the patient chart with great strokes and punchy periods, then looks up to him. "You'll be out of here soon enough. You should enjoy the special treatment while you can."

Mitch's face turns as red, as if he'd been out on the mountain during a blizzard overnight. He grumbles something under his breath. Nurse Lady ignores him completely. She hands the patient chart to another nurse, helps Mitch into his wheelchair, then takes control behind the wheels. Something tells me she's enjoying her present reign of power. I follow behind them, carrying Mitch's suitcase of belongings.

Once we get downstairs, the nurse helps him out of the wheelchair and attempts to walk him to the car.

"I can go on from here," he says, making it perfectly clear she will not be walking him the rest of the way. Other people are milling around, and

Mitch is much too athletic and physical to appear the invalid. Her chin lifts with her eyebrows. She swivels around on her rubber soles then pads off without another word.

He looks at me. "That woman takes her job far too seriously."

Now there's the pot calling the kettle black. We both laugh.

He stops at the door of the car and takes a deep breath.

"Are you all right?"

"I just had to take a deep breath of freedom." He grins, opens the door and climbs inside.

"You've been here less than twenty-four hours, and you act as though you've been in prison for a decade." I switch on the engine, pull out of the hospital pickup area and into traffic.

"I hate being dependent upon someone else." He turns to me. "Now you know one of my greatest weaknesses."

I lift a smile. "Somehow I always suspected that about you."

"You did? What made you think that?"

"I don't know," I say, stopping at a light. "Maybe the fact that you've started your own business and work at it so hard shows me you're a doer. Most doers prefer to handle things themselves, and don't like waiting around for other people."

He sighs. "I suppose it's a pride issue. I'm working on it, but I've got a long ways to go."

"I understand all about that."

"You do?"

"Yeah."

"So, I've told you my weakness. What's yours?"

I'm not enjoying the way this conversation is going.

"Come on. Let's play fair here," he teases.

"My weakness, hmm."

"Quit stalling."

I smile again. "All right, I'll tell you. I'm not into being stretched from my comfort zone."

He studies me a minute. "Really? Your move here would suggest otherwise."

"You assume that was an easy decision for me?"

"Well, wasn't it?"

"No. Your sister forced me into it."

He laughs. "She is good at that, I will admit." We both fall silent a moment. "I'm glad she talked you into it, though."

"Yeah, I can make a pretty mean cappuccino. Well—sometimes."

"I think you know it's more than that," he says, his husky voice in place.

Oh, no, you don't, Mitch Windsor. I'll not fall prey to your charm this time.

"So, you're not going to try and work today, are you?" I quickly change the subject and see the surprise on his face.

"Um, no. I thought I would wait until tomorrow. But at least I'll be around if anyone needs me."

"Oh, I forgot to tell you that Monica called last night to check on you," I say nonchalantly, turning left at the stop sign.

"Yeah, she called me."

I'm not sure what else to say, and he offers no more explanation.

We ride the rest of the way back in silence.

When I pull up to the B and B, Monica is waiting with open arms. No sooner has the car stopped than she is at Mitch's door. He pulls himself out of the car, and she throws her arms around him.

"Mitch, I'm so glad you're all right." To my horror, she reaches up to kiss him, but he turns away. I suppose he's embarrassed in front of me. I hurry toward the door.

I think I hear him call my name, but I keep moving. I can't stand any more humiliation today. It's enough that she's told me they're engaged. I don't need them both to tell me together.

I want to go home.

I'll finish out the week here, but I'm telling Mitch

by day's end of my plans. He's feeling better, and he obviously doesn't need me hanging around.

Once I get to my room, I sit on my bed and cry. My head starts to throb once again. It would be a luxury to wallow in self-pity, but I don't have time. Lisa has to leave, and I need to get to the coffee shop and relieve her of her duties.

I wash my face and head out the door.

"Gwen, I need to talk to you," Mitch says.

"I'll have to talk to you tonight, Mitch. Lisa has to get to class, and she can't leave until I show up." Without giving him time to comment, I'm out the door.

The afternoon drags on forever. Business is down—again. Monica is probably running another special. No doubt, she's proving her point to Mitch. They'd be much better off joining forces rather than working against one another. My headache is better, though I can still feel it on the fringes.

By the time my workday has ended, I've made up my mind. There is no point in me sticking around any longer. I'm making life miserable for everyone. Granny will be glad to get rid of me and Guacamole. Mitch can enjoy Monica, get a replacement for me—one who causes him less grief—and I can go back to Tumbleweed where I belong. For some reason, that thought alone makes every step I take harder than the last.

Thankfully, when I enter the B and B, Granny and Mitch are nowhere to be found. I rush up to my room, gather my things in my suitcase and quickly pack everything into my car. I notice that Mitch's car is gone, so no doubt he has taken Granny to the grocery. It's a perfect time for my escape.

On the last trip to my room, I gather up Guacamole and put him in his small cage. He hates it, but he'll have to learn to cope like the rest of us.

I enter the house once more, scribble out a note of thanks for the opportunity to work there, express my regrets for having to leave but indicate that I feel it's much better for everyone if Guacamole and I go home. I leave the note on the dinner table, knowing they'll see it there.

Once inside my car, I pull out of the B and B so I can be gone before Mitch and Granny get home. I punch Lauren's cell phone number and ask her if I can see her before I leave town. She wants me to stay a couple of days. I want to go home, but I know it will be another year before I can see her again, so I agree.

My resolve to go home begins to wane by the time I arrive at Woods Inn Bed and Breakfast. When I reach the front door, I have a lump in my throat the size of Lake Tahoe. Lauren opens the door, takes one look at my face and pulls me inside.

"Oh, Gwen, you poor thing." She pulls me into her arms and tears sting my eyes. "It's going to be all right."

My throat refuses to set any words free. I finally calm down and pull away from Lauren. The scent of a nearby cinnamon candle makes me feel better.

"Follow me, and I'll show you where you can put your things," Lauren says.

Before long, Guacamole and my things are in a guest room, and Lauren and I are sipping coffee in her great room in front of the fireplace. I've told her my story. Every part of it. My feelings for Mitch. His feelings for Monica. The business. Everything. When I'm completely finished, she doesn't say anything and that makes me nervous.

"Do you think I'm immature?" I ask, my teeth tugging on my lower lip.

"Why would you say that?"

"Oh, I don't know. Maybe I shouldn't have run off like that. I couldn't take another minute there, especially with Monica struttin' her stuff." I look up at Lauren. "All right, so that was an immature comment."

She laughs. "I think you're giving up too soon, Gwen."

"Hardly. Monica told me they're practically engaged. Do I want to stick around for the ceremony?"

"But you know how Monica is. She could be telling you that to get you out of the picture." Lauren takes a drink of coffee.

"I don't think so. Besides, the truth is, I love Mitch too much to stick around. I'm no good for him. I've worked through my vertigo, and I can even ski a little bit, but I'm a klutz, and there's that whole thing with Guacamole. As if those aren't enough, there's that little deal about him not loving me."

"How do you know he doesn't love you?"

"Well, the fact that he hangs out with Monica and hasn't given me any indication to feel that he does love me might be a good clue."

"He's kissed you."

"So what? He's a player, remember."

"In his old days, according to Candace. Have you talked to her about all this?"

I shake my head. "How can I? He's her brother. I don't want to put her in the middle of this." Besides, I think he's got her fooled, too.

"Good point." Lauren makes a face. "I think we need to pray about it. However it turns out, you want to be in the center of the Lord's will."

"That's true. I've finally learned my lesson on that one."

"Took me a while to learn that one, too." Lauren laughs. "Let's pray."

By the time she's finished, I have goose bumps and the assurance that God will get me through this, come what may.

Chapter Twenty-One

No sooner do we finish praying, than someone knocks on the front door. Laura answers and it's Granny.

"Is Gwen Sandler here?" Granny asks Lauren.

Lauren hesitates. I suppose she's not sure if I want her to know. I edge around the corner and step into the hallway so they can see me.

"Hi, Granny," I say, acting as though everything is fine.

She puts her hands on her hips. "You left before Mitch got to talk to you about Guacamole."

Great. She came over here to tell me I'm fired. "I'm sorry. It seemed the best way to handle it. You and Mitch were gone, and I didn't want to wait around."

"Well, if you hadn't been in such an all-fired hurry, you might have learned a thing or two."

Lauren looks at me wide-eyed, and I almost laugh.

"We didn't have a chance to tell you that we know how Guacamole is getting loose from your room."

So they found a hole or something. Does she have to come here and gloat?

"I've been doing a little spying, and I happened to see that housekeeper girl—Kaci what's-her-name—luring Guacamole out of your room with a treat."

"Kaci?" I roll the news around in my mind, but I can't grasp it. "What possible reason would she have for doing that?"

Granny smiles here and shows her perfectly even dentures. "That's where things get interesting. See, when Kaci saw me, she shoved the door closed, and Guacamole stayed inside. I didn't confront her then. I figured I'd tell Mitch first and let him decide what to do. I told him what I saw, and we left for Kaci's house, to get to the bottom of things. She told us that Monica had hired her to do the dirty work. She said Monica wanted to sabotage Mitch's business. You left before we got back."

I gasp here. I can't help it. "Why would Monica have her do that?"

"To get you out of the picture. I guess she figured you were a threat."

"A threat? Me? Why would she think that?"

Granny gives a dramatic sigh here. "For crying out loud, do I have to spell it all out for you?"

I stare at her blankly, having no clue where she's going with this.

"She's in love with Mitch."

Well, there's a no-brainer.

"He's in love with you. And she wants you out of the picture, so she can try to lure—"

"Wait. What did you say?" I see Lauren smiling.

Granny blinks. "I said she's in love with Mitch."

"No, that other part."

"He's in love with you?" Granny looks confused.

"Yeah, that's the one." I mentally wallow in those words a moment.

Granny smiles. "That's what I said. It doesn't take a rocket scientist to figure that one out. Why do you think I put you through domestic boot camp?"

"Huh?"

"The twenty questions, remember? The cooking instructions, scripture reading, all that?"

My mouth is gaping.

"Because I wanted to make sure you knew how to be a good wife. I wanted to make sure you knew the Scriptures and would be a good match for my grandson. He's been through enough with wild women. He needed a good match this time."

Am I dreaming here? I don't know what Granny is doing in my dreams, but I know I'll wake up any minute. I stand mute. Granny walks over to me and grabs my arm. "Are you all right?"

I'm thinking this is the part where I wake up. I'll see Guacamole crawling across my bed and realize I'm at Lauren's B and B.

Granny shakes my arm. "Gwen, are you all right?"

She's squeezing my arm too tight. "Ouch," I say.

Granny tosses a mischievous grin. "See, you're not dreaming."

I gape again. She reads my thoughts. This woman is a wonder.

"There's more. You won't like this part."

Uh-oh, I knew this was too good to be true.

"Lisa was working for her, too."

"What? Lisa was working for whom?"

"Miss Fancy Pants herself."

"Monica?"

"Bingo! You win the prize." Granny's practically rocking on her heels here.

"How do you know?"

"She went to Mitch and told him. Probably couldn't live with the guilt anymore," Granny said.

I feel as though I've fallen facedown in the

snow. How is this possible? She is my friend. We've laughed and talked together, gone places. This just hurts.

"Don't take it too bad. She fooled all of us." Granny's voice has taken on a nurturing sound to it. I should record it. It may not happen again.

"You gonna be all right?" Lauren asks, searching my face.

"Yeah. I'm just a little stunned, is all."

Granny's practical side is back in place. Without further ado, she brushes her hands as though the matter is settled and heads for the door. She turns back to me. "What time can you get back there?"

I swallow hard. "I'm not coming back, Granny."

"Well, forevermore," she says with obvious astonishment. "Why not?"

I shake my head. I don't want to get into all this with Granny. "I really don't think I should." It's the best explanation I can give her. If she can't see that I'm a menace to his business, she truly is blind. Besides, if Mitch wanted me back, if he truly loved me, he would come and tell me himself. He wouldn't send Granny.

Granny's eyes light up. "You're a stubborn little thing, aren't you?" She points her gnarled finger my way. "Well, don't wait too long. I'm tired and I want to stop that kitchen work."

The woman is obviously not understanding me here. "I'm not coming, Granny. You need to find someone else to help you." Why isn't she getting this?

Granny's already heading out the door. "I'll see you soon," she calls over her shoulder and disappears outside.

I'm totally stumped, and I'm sure my expression shows it. Lauren looks at me and laughs. "That woman won't take no for an answer."

"Obviously," I say, feeling confused.

"Come on." Lauren hooks her arm into mine and leads me toward my room. "I think you could use a good night's sleep."

Once I'm ready for bed and beneath my covers, I stare in the darkness toward the ceiling. Every car door I hear tonight gives me hope that Mitch is coming for me, but every time I'm disappointed.

I punch my pillow and try to get comfortable. I may as well give it up. This is how it's meant to be. I was stupid to fall in love with this guy in the first place. We are total opposites. Besides, I don't fit in here. I'm a creature of warmth. I hate the cold. Okay, so I've gotten used to it, but still.

I close my eyes and will myself to slip into a world of dreams. A place where Mitch and I are happy together. A place where Monica Howell does not exist.

Hey, this is *my* dream. I can do what I want.

To say I'm disappointed that Mitch doesn't contact me over the next week is an understatement. Lauren talked me into staying with her that long and, deep down, I had hoped that would give Mitch time to contact me, in case Granny was right.

Obviously, she wasn't. It's time for me to go home.

"I wish you'd stay a few more days, Gwen," Lauren says while we sit in the great room together.

"Thanks, Lauren. I appreciate your kindness, I really do. But it's time for me to go home."

The sad look on her face puts a knot in my throat. She knows this is hard for me.

"If you're sure."

"I'm sure." I muster up a smile. "Hey, enough of this sulking! Mitch isn't exactly the only bear on the mountain."

Lauren suddenly laughs. "Only you could think of that." She stares at me a moment. "You'll be okay?"

"I'll be fine," I assure her, praying it will be so.

"Just promise me you won't settle for Herbert."

"I promise." I flash my finest grin, hoping it will hide the ache in my heart. "You know, I haven't heard from Mom and Dad in a while," I say, wanting desperately to change the subject.

"They're probably enjoying their newfound freedom."

Freedom from me?

She must see the question in my eyes. "With their retirement and all," she quickly adds.

I nod. "Well, I'd better start packing so I can get on the road." We both get up.

"Do you need any help?"

"No, thanks," I say, heading for my room. I hear the phone ring, but the sound fades as I close my door. I have my suitcase nearly packed when Lauren knocks.

"Candace is on the phone. She wants to talk to you."

I hope she doesn't try to smooth things over. I really don't want to talk about it.

"Hello?"

"Hey, kiddo! I had to call and thank you for helping my brother."

Well, that's not exactly what I want to hear. She's thanking me for leaving?

She must notice my silence here. "As you know, his business has been down. Normally, he gives up when things get too tough, and he flits to the next thing. Not this time. Thanks to you, he came up with a brilliant idea."

My spirits perk up a tiny bit here.

"You see, our uncle is a retired art teacher, and he used to compete in ice-sculpture competitions. Mitch talked to him, and Uncle Fred is going to offer ice-sculpting classes at the resort and hold occasional competitions to drum up business. Mitch is getting fliers printed up. Some of the radio stations in town are getting excited about it. Mitch is working with them and Uncle Fred on dates for the competitions and having the stations come out for a day of food and fun. He's hoping to get the whole town involved! I think this will really work!"

Candace's enthusiasm is catching. I'm excited for her and Mitch. "That's great, Candace."

"Isn't it?" She barely pauses for breath here. "But that's not all. Our parents are so proud of how he's handling things by not giving up and truly proving to them that he's changed, and now they're offering their financial support. They want to partner in the business so he can expand things. They see things really taking off for Mitch."

"That's wonderful. So will Monica close her business to join him?" I ask.

"What are you talking about?"

I explain what Monica had expressed to me.

"And you believed all that, Gwen?" Candace sounds incredulous.

"I found it hard to believe at first, but she was so persuasive. And Mitch hasn't exactly made me feel otherwise. I couldn't get past thinking that maybe this time she was right."

"Look, Gwen, I don't know why my brother hasn't contacted you, but you can be sure it's not because of Monica Howell. In fact, I know he pretty much told her if he found her snooping around his business again, he would call the authorities."

I'm not sure what to say. So the engagement is off. Maybe Mitch cares for me a little, but I have no commitment from him, and the truth is I don't want to stick around and eventually get hurt again.

"You're going home, aren't you?"

"I have to, Candace. I can't wait around here forever."

"Do you love him?"

Her question startles me.

"Well, do you?"

"Yes."

"If it's the right thing, God will help you two to work it out."

Lauren comes to my door. "Gwen, there's someone here to see you." My heart leaps to my throat.

"I've got to go, Candace. Someone is here for me."

"I'll be praying for you, Gwen."

"Thanks. Bye."

With my heart in my throat, I walk to the front door. Mitch is standing there with his hat in his gloved hands. "Hi, Gwen." His gaze holds mine.

"Hi."

"I wanted to let you know that your parents are at the B and B."

"What?" That's the last thing I expected to hear.

He swallows hard. "They just showed up, asking for you. They're planning to stay there in the motor home for a couple of nights."

Great. I can't let them know I'm headed back to Tumbleweed, or they'll think I'm giving up. Worse than that, they'll think they have to stop their traveling plans to make me feel better. I won't get this past Mom. She'll know something's going on, and she'll refuse to leave me. I have to keep my spirits up for them.

"I didn't know if you would still want to work for me while they are there or not."

Mitch has guessed my dilemma.

"I suppose that will give you more time to look for someone," I say as though I'm doing him the favor, when the truth is that he's helping me.

His eyes brighten. "That's right."

We both know I don't have much choice in the matter, but pride holds me still for a moment.

"The truth is I want you to come back," Mitch says, his gaze never leaving my face.

Well, why didn't you say so? "You do?"

He takes a step closer to me, his gaze still fixed on me. He stops, his fingers still working the hat. "Yes, I do."

"Okay, I'll come—but only for as long as my parents are there." As much as I want to stay longer, I can't. Granny and Candace tell me he cares, but *he* hasn't said it. Until he does, my plans to go home are unchanged.

Something flickers in his eyes. Disappointment, or is that wishful thinking on my part?

"I didn't tell your parents where you were, of course. I told them you were gone for a little while. Will you return soon?"

"I'm packed. I'll be there in ten minutes," I say with a guarded smile.

"Listen, Gwen, I'm sorry I haven't been more trusting about things. Guacamole's escapes—well, everything." He looks down at his hat, moving it between his fingers. "There's no excuse for it when you've been nothing but supportive, but I had a good friend betray me once in a business deal, and I've struggled with trust ever since."

I don't know what to say.

"Well, anyway, I'll look forward to seeing you back at the inn."

Mitch turns and leaves, and I quickly tell Lauren all that Candace said.

"Don't give up hope yet, Gwen. Something tells me your life is about to drastically change." She smiles.

"Like it hasn't already?" I tease. A somber feeling takes over. "I don't want to get my hopes up, Lauren. However it turns out, I'll be fine. The Lord will get me through."

She gives me a hug and I leave, wondering what this day will bring.

Chapter Twenty-Two

"Hi, Mom, Dad!" I throw my arms first around my mother, then give my dad a big hug.

"How's our girl?" Dad asks.

"I'm good." I don't want the conversation directed at me. "And look at the two of you. You look wonderful," I say, flashing my best smile. "This new lifestyle obviously agrees with you."

Dad puts his arm around Mom's waist. "We are having a great time, Gwen."

Mom actually blushes here. "We've had such fun seeing the sights and getting reacquainted." She gives Dad a smile, and they get all mushy with each other. It's kind of sickening. I think I'm jealous.

"By the way, I got a look at your new boss." Mom's eyebrows wiggle here. "Quite the catch, I would say. And yes, I did notice he has a naked ring finger." She winks.

Leave it to Mom to notice. "He's a nice man, Mom, but, as you say, he's my boss, nothing more." Maybe he's not interested in Monica, if Granny and Candace are right, but he's not interested in me in that way, either, or he would have told me.

Mom puts her arm around my waist and ushers me toward their motor home. "Well, time will tell, dear. Time will tell." I get the sneaking suspicion she knows something I don't. But then Mom always acts that way when it comes to my love life—or lack thereof. As though God has made her privy to something about me. No doubt she sees grandchildren on the horizon.

I can only hope Polyester Man is nowhere to be seen.

Once I get Mom and Dad settled in, I spend the rest of that day and the following day interviewing possible managers for Cool Beanz. I've finally made a decision on one. Cool Beanz is closed, and Mitch is meeting me in a few minutes to discuss the new manager.

I hope to talk to Lisa someday about everything, but it hurts too much right now. Mitch says she desperately needed tuition money for school, and Monica paid a pretty price for information. Lisa told Mitch she felt horrible about it and that she would make it up to him somehow. She wrote me a letter of apology, saying she never expected our friendship to develop like it did. I forgive her, but still, I can't talk to her yet. Maybe after I'm home, I'll write to her and tell her how I feel.

To say I'm nervous to meet with Mitch is an understatement. He has pretty much avoided me— or is it the other way around?—since I've returned. Granny and Candace obviously had their facts wrong. I'm sick of heart, but I know I'll adjust. It may take years, a lifetime maybe, but I'll make it.

At this point, I want to hurry up and get the new woman hired so I can go home. My parents plan to leave in the morning, so I'll be ready to head out right after they leave. I figure I can make it that long.

The door squeaks open, and the evening chill swishes inside. Mitch closes the door behind him.

I pull on my professional side and grab the folder with employee applications, my manager pick at the top of the stack.

Mitch declines anything to drink, so I figure he wants to get right down to business. I zip through the applicants, then show him my pick, explaining my position. He agrees. For some reason, that makes me sad. I realize my position is truly over, and this place will soon be but a memory.

"Well, you've done a good job, and I think she will do fine, Gwen." He stands from the table.

This is it. He'll be out the door tomorrow morning and probably won't even say goodbye. Mitch Windsor will breeze out of my life as quickly as he entered it. I struggle with the tears stinging my eyes.

"Do you have any plans right now?"

I blink.

"Tonight, were you going anywhere?"

I reluctantly shake my head.

"Great." He reaches for my coat. "Will you come with me?" He holds it open and I blindly stand, wondering what we're doing. He helps me into my coat and grabs my hand, leading me out the door.

"What are we doing? Where are we going?" Despite my confusion, excitement bubbles up inside me. I try to contain it. I don't want to get hurt anymore.

"You ask too many questions, you know that?" He laughs and guides me out of the shop. I lock the door. We grab the ski lift, ride down the slope in silence, and at the base there is a sleigh and horses waiting for us.

"What is this?"

"Horses," he says, pointing to the two brown creatures that are snorting and pawing the ground in an effort to keep warm. "Sleigh," he says, pointing.

I can't help but smile. He extends his hand to me to help me onto the sleigh. Glistening stars poke through a velvety sky while a full moon sails high above the treetops.

Mitch climbs aboard the sleigh and with a flick of the reins, we're on our way. To where, I have no idea. The whisper of horses' hooves sounds across the snow-laden path as we roam down forgotten roads in silence. I suspect he's gathering his nerve to tell me goodbye.

"I need to talk to you, and this seems to be the only way I can get you alone." Mitch finally maneuvers the team near the side of the road and pulls the horses to a stop. He turns to me, the moonlight full on his face, dancing in his eyes.

He reaches behind him for something then turns to me with a dozen red roses in his hands. He had them in some protective wrap so I couldn't see them when I boarded.

A gasp sticks in my throat. I take a whiff from the petals and close my eyes, willing the moment to never end. I look at him and open my mouth to say something.

He holds up his hand. "Before you say anything, let me speak my piece."

I'm all ears. The serious expression on his face makes me place the roses beside me on the seat.

"Candace called me today. She said she told you all about my uncle and how my parents are on the bandwagon to help me."

I smile. "I'm very happy for you, Mitch."

He grabs my hands. "I couldn't have done it without you, Gwen." A sparkle enters his eyes, and I suddenly realize the roses are a thank-you, nothing more.

He tells me all about his plans for the business, how I gave him the courage to venture out and try something new. His words ride on the fringes of the breeze, and I barely take notice. I hear only the quiet beating of my heart, a lonely single beat. I'm happy for him, I really am. I only wish we were forging the future together.

"Did you hear what I said?"

My eyes focus on him.

"I said, I couldn't have done it without you, nor can I do it without you."

I'm not understanding.

"Gwen, I had to prove to myself that I could stick with something, that I could make a life for myself, provide for a family. You see, my parents weren't the only ones who didn't trust me. I didn't trust myself. I knew that God had done work in my life, but I was still afraid I would blow it."

He has my full attention now.

"You stretched out of your comfort zone to come here. How you handled the vertigo, everything, has amazed me and given me the courage to step out myself. You see, I could be adventurous about things that didn't really matter. But settling down, committing to one thing—that was an adventure I wasn't sure I could handle."

I'm afraid to breathe here. My whole future hinges on his next words.

He squeezes my hands tighter and stares straight into my soul. "Gwen Sandler, I fell in love with you the moment I held you in my arms after your first vertigo attack, remember?"

Like I could forget. I wish I could have focused more on him holding me, but that's just hard to do when your world is spinning. Wait. Did he say "fell in love with you"? As in fell in love with me? Him and me? G&M, together? Okay, I like where this is going. I sit up a little taller, but not too tall because his face is still quite serious here.

"I know I don't have the best reputation in town. I'm sure you've heard about my past with women. I can be pigheaded, and I know that we have different interests, but do you think you could ever…what I mean to say is…is there any possibility that you would consider—"

His whispered words ride softly on the breeze and make their way to my heart. I put my hand on his lips. "I love you, Mitch Windsor."

The moonlight encircles his face, and my heart flutters with his smile. He pulls me into the circle of his arms, his lips touching mine in a way that tells me I belong to him and him alone.

He pulls away and looks at me. "I know we've only known each other a couple of months, and I can wait as long as you need, if you'll only promise me that one day you will be my wife."

His tender words make me cry. I can't help it. If I'm dreaming here, woe unto the person who tries to wake me up!

His hand reaches up and gently wipes the tears from my face. "I love you, Gwen Sandler. Will you marry me?"

I throw my arms around him. "Yes, yes, a thousand times, yes!" I squeeze him with everything in me. He coughs and I release my hold.

"Remind me to let you win our arguments. You've got a mean squeeze there," he teases.

"Trust me, I will." I throw in a laugh.

"Oh, one more thing."

Uh-oh, here it comes. I brace myself.

"I don't even care if you want to wear a red wedding dress."

Okay, that idea has potential, but I can imagine the horror on my mother's face right here. I'll have to stick with traditional hues to keep everyone happy. "Maybe I'd better keep the red tucked inside my bridal bouquet."

Mitch arches an eyebrow. "Peacemaker, eh?"

I smile. The magnitude of everything hits me. "What about Monica?"

"She blew everything way out of proportion. I told you that you can't trust her. She constantly concocted ways for us to get together, always offering business connections or valuable information that I thought could help my business. It was always about that, and she knew that was the only way I would see her. At first I thought she was really trying to help. Once I realized she was going for something more, I told her that my heart belonged to someone else, and she would never be more than a friend and business acquaintance."

I try not to mentally throw the balloons here. I really do, but I just can't stop myself. Suddenly, I remember that my parents are here. "We have to tell my parents!" I say, excitedly.

"Well, I already did."

I'm speechless.

"I had to ask your dad for your hand in marriage."

Have I mentioned that I love this guy?

"I assume Dad and Mom gave you their blessings?" I ask with confidence.

"Yes, they did. In fact, your mom's first words to me were, 'How do you feel about children?' What's that about?"

I groan. "Let's go back to the house, and I'll tell you all about it…."

We make our way to the B and B, and I explain my mother's desperate desire for grandchildren. Our laughter rings out through the night air. Mitch pulls me close, and I snuggle in beside him. I take a deep breath, gaze up at the shining stars and whisper a *thank-you* in my heart.

God is in control of my life. He always has been and always will be. And you know what? There's no other place I'd rather be than in the center of His will.

Okay, and if His will includes living my life at a ski resort alongside the man of my dreams, hey, who am I to complain?

* * * * *

Dear Reader,

I had never skied a day in my life when I decided to write this story. So, I trudged up to Michigan and proceeded to take my first ski lesson. I'm sorry to report my experience was no better than Gwen Sandler's experience. In fact, I'm surprised I survived the whole ordeal. Our friends are making plans for next year. I feel a headache coming on....

In my story, Gwen lived her life to please others, but there came a day when she had to step out of her familiar cocoon and make a life for herself—the life she felt God had intended for her.

Mitch Windsor had lived a carefree, selfish life—at the expense of others—until God showed him a better way.

While writing Gwen and Mitch's story, I was reminded once again how God in my life makes all the difference.

Psalm 37:4 says to "Delight yourself in the Lord, and He will give you the desires of your heart."

He is an awesome God who loves you and wants you to delight in Him! How cool is that? He wants to guide you along life's pathway, give you a future and a hope!

So if you're trudging aimlessly through your days, wondering what your life is all about; delight in Him. He can make a difference in your life, in your family, in your world.

God bless,

Diann

QUESTIONS FOR DISCUSSION

1. Sometimes we get comfortable in our lives and change doesn't come easily. That's what happened to Gwen Sandler. Have there been times in your own life when you struggled with a job change, a move, or someone in your life moving elsewhere? If so, what happened? If not, how do you think you would handle it if you did have a major change in your life?

2. Gwen handled her frustrations with chocolate and prayer. How do you handle yours?

3. Gwen accepted the position at the ski resort, knowing she had vertigo. Do you think she did the right thing by staying there and facing her fears, or do you think she should have gone back home when she realized what would be required of her? What would you have done?

4. Do you think that sometimes it's good to be pushed out of your comfort zone? Why or why not?

5. Gwen and Mitch both struggled with trust issues. If your best friend's character suddenly came into question, how would you handle it?

6. Do you have a friend who has failed you as Lisa Jamison did Gwen? How did it make you feel? Are you willing to forgive them? Why or why not?

7. Sometimes we learn the most during the hardest times. If you have been betrayed by someone close to you, have you allowed it to make you bitter or better? How has that reaction affected your life?

8. How have you proved yourself to be a trustworthy friend to others?

9. Gwen's positive approach to life seemed to get her through the tough times. Do you look at the world through "negative eyes," or do you choose to see the best in others? Do you choose to make the best of life's difficulties? How has your response to difficulties affected your life and others around you?